Mark Guy Pearse

Daniel Quorm

And His Religious Notions. Second Series

Mark Guy Pearse

Daniel Quorm
And His Religious Notions. Second Series

ISBN/EAN: 9783337129460

Printed in Europe, USA, Canada, Australia, Japan

Cover: Foto ©Raphael Reischuk / pixelio.de

More available books at **www.hansebooks.com**

DANIEL QUORM,

AND

HIS RELIGIOUS NOTIONS.

SECOND SERIES.

BY

MARK GUY PEARSE,

AUTHOR OF "MISTER HORN AND HIS FRIENDS," ETC.

ILLUSTRATED BY CHARLES TRESIDDER.

THIRTIETH THOUSAND.

London:

T. WOOLMER, 2, CASTLE STREET, CITY ROAD, E.C.
AND 66, PATERNOSTER ROW, E.C.

1884.

Contents

OF THE SECOND SERIES.

Dan'el goes to see Frankey Vivian.

POOR old Frankey Vivian was sinking fast. Shaken by his cough and with failing breath, he now sat propped with pillows. His features were pinched, and a look of exhaustion had settled on his face, yet the old light and joy shone out more radiant than ever. The long years of climbing as a miner, the foul air of deep underground, and the quick change from the heat to the bleak winds that swept the surface, had nearly done their work. He could be with his friends on earth but a little while longer, a few days at most.

Daniel Quorm was a daily visitor, sitting by the bedside for an hour or more; the bright eye that looked over the broad-rimmed spectacles often dimmed with tears. But it was Frankey who with husky and broken voice was speaking now. The wasted hand was held out toward Dan'el; and as he spoke a strange, new vigour came into his voice and manner.

"A little while, my dear leader; only a little while, an' I shall be at home. Why, it makes me feel quite well again for to think about it. Last night I was lyin' somehow 'tween sleepin' an' wakin', I s'pose 'twas a kind of a dream, but I could see the old friends a-lookin' out for me. There's old Uncle Jem Polsue—he has been up there goin' on for two year; he's keepin' a look out for me, I know. An' so is the old Mestur Trewhela. It seemed to me like as if I could a'most hear them talkin'."

"Bless thee, dear Frankey, thou 'rt near enough to hear them, I do believe," said Dan'el very softly.

"Seemin' to me," Frankey went on, "that I could see old Uncle Jem comin' along the golden Street, an' up come Mest' Trewhela, an' shakes hands with him.

"'How are 'e, Sir?' says Uncle Jem.

"'Wonderful,' says Mest' Trewhela, 'wonderful; never so well in all my life. How are you, Uncle Jem?'

"Says Uncle Jem : ' How am I, Mest' Trewhela, how am I ! why, I do hardly know myself : an' I've a-got to keep on saying,—Be you the old Jem Polsue from down there to Bray—be you ? 'Cause *he* had got rheumatics dreadful, he had—an' *you* can fly right round the world for your Blessed Lord, an' never so much as feel it. Why, *he* hadn't scarce any breath—an' *you* can go praisin' the glorious Lord day an' night in His holy temple. It can't be you, sure 'nough, Uncle Jem. But 'tis, bless the Lord—'tis, an' no mistake. That's how I be, Mest' Trewhela, 'zactly.'

" ' Well,' says Mest' Trewhela, ' seen anybody from down our way lately, have 'e, Uncle Jem ? '

" ' No,' says Uncle Jem, ' I haven't, Mest' Trewhela. But I been thinkin' that 'tis most time for the poor old Frankey Vivian to be comin' up here, isn't it ? '

" ' Iss, Jem, iss,' says Mest' Trewhela. ' He's bound to be up here before very long. How he will praise the Blessed Lord when he do get his breath again ! '

" And I lifted up my voice and cried out,—'I'm comin', my dear comrades—Hallelujah !' And I woke myself up with blessin' the Lord. Sing, Dan'el—sing."

And Frankey's voice was choked as a fit of coughing came on. Presently Dan'el rang out the

old favourite tune, ' Jerusalem,' whilst Frankey put
in a trembling note now and then, lifting his hand
in time with the tune, and in his complete enjoyment of the words :

> " And let this feeble body fail,
>   And let it droop and die ;
> My soul shall quit the mournful vale,
>   And soar to worlds on high.

> " Surely He will not long delay :
>   I hear His Spirit cry,
> ' Arise, My love, make haste away !
>   Go, get thee up, and die.'

> " O what hath Jesus bought for me !
>   Before my ravished eyes
> Rivers of life Divine I see,
>   And trees of paradise ;

> " I see a world of spirits bright
>   Who reap the pleasures there ;
> They all are robed in purest white,
>   And conquering palms they bear.

> " They drink the vivifying stream,
>   They pluck the ambrosial fruit,
> And each records the praise of Him
>   Who tuned his golden lute.

> " O what are all my sufferings here,
>   If, Lord, Thou count me meet
> With that enraptured host to appear,
>   And worship at Thy feet ! "

" ' Worship at *Thy feet !* ' gasped Frankey.
" *Thy feet !* my Blessed Lord ; " and with his hands
clasped and his face shining with joy, he looked as

if the gates of the celestial city were flung open
just before him and he were gazing straight in.

Then Dan'el turned to the Bible. It was opened
at the twenty-third Psalm. With a strange depth
of tenderness the rugged old shoemaker began
to speak of it, staying to let Frankey drink in the
rich meaning, and interspersing it with his own
comments.

" *The Lord*—so it begins, Frankey. We must
get up very high before we can start. 'Tis too
high for you an' me, I'm 'fraid. *The Lord !* why,
the earth is His and the fulness thereof. *The
Lord !* why, His name is called 'Wonderful, Coun-
sellor, The Mighty God, The Everlasting Father,
The Prince of Peace.' Come, David, what great
thing hast thou to say o' this glorious Lord ? "

Dan'el turned again to the Bible, the short,
sturdy forefinger guiding his eye. " *The Lord is my*
—*my*, hear that, old friend—that this mighty Lord
should know anything o' you or me, or should care
for us. My what, David ?—my King ? my Redeemer ? my Judge ? my God ? *The Lord is my
Shepherd.* Ah ! that brings Him down right close
to us, Frankey. *Shepherd !* why, how homely it
makes Him ! doesn't it ? You an' I *can* start along
with Him, and go all the way too, Frankey."

" Bless Him," whispered Frankey, feasting on
the words. ' *My* Shepherd ! why, 'tis like as if He'd

only got one sheep to care for, an' that one is me. My Shepherd."   .

"So 'tis, dear Frankey. I'm fine an' glad for thy sake. An' then, you see, there's one thing He's bound to do. A shepherd may please hisself about a hundred things: he may look after his bit o' garden, or see to his house; but he *must* look after his sheep—*must*. He can't anyhow please hisself about that."

Again the sharp eye turned to the Bible, and there was a moment's silence.

"But stop, Frankey. I forgot that; an' I often think about it too. We must begin at the beginnin'. This is a Psalm of David; so it do say. I do like that. I've seen a lovely picture of a very fine young gentleman all dressed out in his best clothes, lyin' in the shade of a tree, among the buttercups an' daisies, playin' music to the birds an' butterflies, an' the sheep scattered about in the prettiest groups you ever saw—and they called it a shepherd. Pooh—all a pack o' moonshine. Like as if the sun never set, an' the wind never blew a gale, an' the rain never came down—like as if the sheep never went astray, an' a pretty figure that young gentleman would be a-climbin' over hedges an' ditches, an' through furze an' bramble! Or like as if there wasn't no wolves an' no robbers. No, this isn't all pipin' an' pictures. 'Tis a Psalm o' David; an' he knew different from that. He knew what it was to drop the harp an' to cudgel a bear. He had come out o' his comfortable corner an' killed a lion, David had. He had gone wanderin' over the moors, clamberin' over the rocks an' down the cliffs in search of the stray sheep, and then he'd come home in the fierce heat carryin' the runaway 'pon his shoulder. He knew the rub of it, an' the work of it, David did—knew what silly things sheep are, an' what a time of it the shepherd have got with 'em sometimes. And he says, *The Lord is my Shepherd.* It means a brave deal more than most folks make out of it, I know."

"Go on, my dear leader," whispered Frankey, as Dan'el paused; "I do dearly love to hear about it."

Dan'el went on again, this time breaking out more cheerily.

"*I shall not want.* Pretty boasting that for a sheep, Frankey, a silly sheep. Hold thy tongue, do, thou vain sheep—why, thou canst not do anything for thyself. Thou canst not run like a hare, or go like a horse, or burrow like a rabbit, or fly like a bird, or hide like even a worm can. Thou hast not got the horns of an ox, nor the heels of an ass. *As for the stork, the fir-trees are her house. The high hills are a refuge for the wild goats; and the rocks for the conies.* But where is thy refuge,

thou poor sheep? Why, there is only one thing in
all the world that thou art clever at : that is, clamberin' over thy Master's hedges an' gettin' into
trouble. Thou ought to be ashamed of thyself,
boastin' like that, for a'most everything can turn
into thy enemy. 'I'll parch thee,' says the summer ;
'I'll bury thee,' says the snow; 'I'll sweep thee
away,' says the flood; 'I'll pick thy eyes out,'
says the raven; 'I'll steal thee,' says the robber ;
'I'll eat thee,' says the wolf."

Then turning to the Book, Dan'el read on with
deep tenderness :

"HE *maketh me to lie down in green pastures ;*
HE *leadeth me.* What! HE leadeth thee! Then
thou art right, sheep, quite right. Boast again, an'
louder still. Summer an' winter, floods an' drought,
wolf an' robber—not one o' them can touch thee :
HE leadeth thee! then thou art safe, sure 'nough. He
will take right good care o' thee, weak as thou art."

"O! Thou art a blessed, blessed Lord," said
Frankey, rapturously.

"*He maketh me to lie down in green pastures.*
That's worth turnin' over for a minute or two,
Frankey. I expect that it do mean the young
green grass when 'tis springin' up all fresh an'
new ; that's what it do say in the margin—pastures
of *tender grass.* There, Frankey, think o' that.
The good Lord do give His sheep the very best.

—Common trade an' poor stuff won't do for His flock at all."

"Just like Him, dear leader. Bless His name," and old Frankey's face shone with joy.

"And then *to lie down* too. Isn't that like Him? I expect that sheep stand up so long as they're hungry, and then when they've had enough they lie down. Ah, He gives His sheep the very best; but not just a taste of it, He *fills* 'em with it. That's like Him, too, isn't it?"

"'Zactly, my dear leader, the *dear* Lord."

"*Beside the still waters.* There's safety, too. Peace an' plenty for thee, Frankey, and then *safety.* No great torrents a-comin' down all of a sudden, sweepin' the poor sheep away before it do know where 'tis.

"Then I do dearly love the next verse. This do seem all so good, just a little bit like the picture; an' when I've got so far as this I can't help sayin', 'Dan'el, there's proper sheep for thee! all so good and lovely. Thou art not like that: so wayward an' wilful as thou art every now an' then.' But then I do come to the next verse: *He restoreth my soul.* There, I see the silly, forgetful sheep go climbin' over the hedge, an' then it goes scrambling down in the lane 'pon the other side, and it do go on and on till 'tis out 'pon the wild moor all lonely an' forlorn, an' it do begin to bleat for the rest, and do wonder where they're a-gone to. Then the good Shepherd looks up, an' He sees directly that one is missin'. He has got plenty here, an' that old wanderer, why, he has gone away so often an' given the Shepherd so much trouble. Besides, he isn't really worth the trouble, so old and torn. But lo! the Blessed Shepherd is gone, over dusty roads an' rocky moors, on, ever so tired, but lookin' an lookin' still, like as if He can't give it up. Then He do catch sight o' it, an' do take it up all so tender, an' do bring it home again, so glad for to have it. Blessed Lord! I do thank Thee for that!" and Dan'el's voice trembled for a moment. "When I come to that I do always say, 'Lord, Thou knowest that old sheep well. He have given Thee ever so much trouble, and he isn't anyhow worth it. An' that old sheep's name is Dan'el Quorm.'"

"'Tis Frankey Vivian, too, dear leader. Bless Him. *He restoreth my soul.*"

"And when He brings us back He can keep us, Frankey. *He leadeth me in the paths of righteousness for His name's sake.*"

"For His *name's sake*," whispered Frankey.

"Yes; that's sure, isn't it? For His very name's sake He leads us in the paths o' righteousness. His name is Jesus, for He shall save His people from their sins. It would be like takin' away His crown for Him not to lead us in the paths o' right-

cousness. He's a tender Shepherd, an' will take
care of His sheep, but He's a wonderful clever
Shepherd, too: for to make us troublesome, forgetful, wanderin' sheep go on in the right path,—
that's something like a Shepherd, isn't it?"

Again Frankey's face beamed with joy, and with
clasped hands and with a strange vigour he burst
out rapturously, "O! blessed, blessed Lord! What
a Saviour Thou art! Wonderful! wonderful!"

Daniel's voice sank into its tone of deepest tenderness as he read on again: "*Yea, though I walk
through the valley of the shadow of death, I will fear
no evil.*"

Then he was silent for so long a time that
Frankey turned toward him appealingly: "Finish
it, my dear leader. Don't 'e leave me in that
dreadful place all alone!"

"I was thinkin', Frankey, what a picture it is,
an' what a brave man this here is. I got it all up
before me the other day so plain as could be. It
was getting late in the evenin', and I was down by
the sea. There was a mist rollin' in, an' it made it
all strange an' ghostly. I was comin' down between
the deep sides o' the valley all alone, and on in front
o' me I could hear the roar o' the ground-swell. I
says to myself, 'Dan'el,' I says, ''tis like the
valley of the shadow of death, all lonely, an' strange,
an' ghostly.'

"And then seemin' to me like as if I could see the man comin' down 'long through the valley. He didn't creep on, an' stop listenin', frightened, an' then go on again a step or two. He didn't come along like as if dreadful hands that you couldn't see were draggin' him down the dark valley. But he marched along all so brave an' happy, singin' so cheerful, like as if he didn't know what fear was. And I wondered if there was anything else in all the world that could make a man go down through the dark valley like that there."

"Bless Him; bless Him," was the only response that Frankey could make.

"Nobody else could help us much if they did go with us, could they, Frankey? They don't know any more about it than we do our own selves. But the Blessed Lord has been down through it, an' He do know the way right out into the light an' glory 'pon the other side. And now He His own self do come back for to take us by the hand. 'Fear not,' says He; 'I will go with thee.' And then our hearts do cry out: 'Lord, I *will* fear no evil, for Thou art with me.' I do fancy, Frankey, that perhaps that night when the disciples were toilin' hard to bring the boat to the land, and they were beginnin' to be afraid because the waves were comin' into the boat, perhaps one o' them said, 'Don't 'ee be 'fraid 't all, comrades.' But all the time the man's own face was pale enough, an' his very voice shook, an' he was so much frightened as anybody. And p'raps some o' the folks ashore saw 'em in the early mornin', an' cried out, 'Don't 'ee be afraid 't all: you'll do it.' Ah, it was all very fine for them to talk like that, when they were safe ashore. But presently there came a very different voice, an' it said: *Be not afraid—it is I.* Then there was a great calm, and they were at land directly."

"*Thou* art with *me,* dear Master," cried Frankey, as his face lit up with joy.

Then Dan'el rose. "Now, old friend, I've talked to thee long enough," and he closed the book; "thou must not have any more than just a word o' prayer."

"Well, thank 'ee, dear leader," said Frankey wistfully; "but I do wish you'd go on a bit more."

"Nay, Frankey; I won't send thee to heaven faster than thou art going, for I shall find it hard work to give thee up. But there—keep the Word in thy heart an' feed 'pon it: '*I will fear no evil : for Thou art with me.*' I thought o' thee the other day down to Redburn—Peter's fair-day it was. There was a lot o' bullocks goin' by with long horns an' fierce eyes, terrible lookin'. A gentleman was comin' along with his little maid, an' when the women folk began to run into the doorways out o' their road, I heard the gentleman say, 'Aren't you

afraid, Jeanie?' And the little maid looked up in
his face and laughed and shook his hand : ' Why,
no, father,' says she, ' o' course not; why, *you're
here, you know.*' Frankey, thou hast got hold o'
the right Hand, and He will keep tight hold o' thine.
Thou canst look death an' hell in the face an' say,
' *I will fear no evil : for Thou art with me.*' "

Frankey gets into Doubting Castle.

GAIN Dan'el sat at Frankey's side. The two or three days that had passed had brought no change, except that the joyous light had gone, and now there was a look of weary sadness, very strange on Frankey's face. The enemy had been harassing the dying man : and to-day the talk was of gloom and doubts.

"Dan'el," Frankey whispered hoarsely, "the old enemy's been at me fierce an' furious. You can't think what dreadful things he do keep tellin' me all night long when I'm lyin' here in the darkness and stillness."

"Bless thee, my dear old Frankey, bless thee," said Dan'el in his tenderest tone, taking the wasted hand in his own; "what a ghastly old coward he is to be sure, to come hittin' a man when he's down, like thou art! But there—'tis just like un—'zactly."

"So 'tis, my dear leader. An' then the dreadful things he do say too! He do come 'pon me like as if from all sides to once. 'Thou art such an old sinner,' says he, 'there's no hope for thee—not a bit. And as for thy wife an' children, they'll starve,' says he. 'And thy faith will fail thee in the dark valley, an' thou wilt be like a man down the shaft with his candle blowed out. An' the Lord Jesus—why, what is an old worn-out sinner like thou art to the King o' Glory?' That roused me, Dan'el, that did." And as Frankey spoke the fire flashed in his eye again, and his voice regained something of its strength. "I lifted myself up then, and says I, 'Devil, if thou art comin' for a wrestle with me I can't do much agen thee. Tell me so much as thou wilt that I am an old sinner, an' I shan't argey with thee a bit—I do give in to that in a minute. Tell me about my wife an' children; I do know that my Heavenly Father will take care o' them. But to come a-tellin' me that my Blessed Lord Jesus don't love me!—no, I can't stand that, an' I won't neither. Weak as I be I can throw 'ee 'pon that ground.' But, my dear leader, I couldn't do it. He kept on so that he tired me out an' laid me right 'pon my back."

Again the light died, and the voice failed him. It was with the hoarse whisper, and staying often to recover his breath, that he went on:

" He kept tellin' me that the Lord Jesus had got something much better to do than for to look after an old man like me. ' You ben't nohow worth it, Frankey Vivian,' says he, ' you do know you ben't; an' there—'tis nothing but conceit a-puffin 'ce up for to think that thou art. He care for *thee!* Why, He have got thousands o' glorious great angels flyin' about for to do His will! Care for *thee!* why, there's this here great world to be looked after, an' such a troublesome world as 'tis too. Why, if He cared for thee, dostn't think He would send an angel for to sit alongside o' thee now an' then, and cheer thee up a bit when Dan'el can't come?' So he kept on till I was down, an' I felt like the horror of a great darkness a-shiverin' me all over."

Then Frankey sank back, faint and wretched.

For a minute or two Dan'el was quiet, lifting up his heart in prayer for guidance. Then he opened the Bible at the eleventh chapter of St. Matthew's Gospel.

" Well, Frankey, bless thee, 'tis a dismal place to be in, sure 'nough, is this same Doubtin' Castle.

But there's one thing—thou art not alone. David
sat down in the same cell, and sang that forty-second
Psalm—*Why art thou cast down, O my soul? and
why art thou disquieted within me?* The old tempter
got him on his back too, Frankey. *As with a
sword in my bones, mine enemies reproach me; while
they say daily unto me, Where is thy God?* And I
reckon that the Blessed Lord Jesus Himself came
very near it some time or other when He was in all
points tempted like as we are. Anyhow, He do come
alongside of us when *we* are there, an' do show us
how to get out. Then there was Elijah—he was a
prisoner there too. But while you was a-talkin' I
thought about another—John the Baptist. I was
readin' about him only a day or two ago. He was
shut up in the same dungeon, Frankey. Now
that's what I do call brave company for 'ee, isn't
it? David, an' Elijah, an' John the Baptist, an'
the Blessed Jesus close by. Why, a'most all the
great men o' the Bible got in here somehow. Come,
Frankey, if you can tell a man by his friends, you
needn't mind goin' to prison in company like that."

Frankey smiled in reply to Dan'el's more cheery
tone. Putting on his big spectacles, Dan'el turned
to the Book and began to read: "*Now when John
had heard in the prison the works of Christ.—In the
prison.* I fancy I do see him there in his dark
dungeon, Frankey. An' these two disciples have

managed to get in to visit him. They're telling about Jesus and the mighty things He is doin' all over the land, an' about the talk there is everywhere, some sayin' one thing about Him and some another. And there do sit John, who never feared man nor devil,—you'd expect to see him like a caged lion. But he sighs,—'Well, I don't know what to think 'bout it 't all,' says John. 'If He really is the great King o' kings, why, I can't help thinkin' that He'd come and take me out o' this here wished old place. You see, I gave up my life to Him, and testified of Him. An' now if He can do these here wonders that Isaiah said He should, why, He could open these prison doors and set this poor captive free.' Poor John, I can hear him sigh again, and he do put his face down between his hands, makin' his chains clank every time he do move.

"Then, Frankey, I expect these two disciples do begin for to try an' comfort their master. But they're wished poor hands at that work; for if John's Saviour hadn't come, nobody else could do much for him."

Frankey shook his head sadly.

"Then if these two disciples were anything like folks are to-day, why, they'd think 'pon a score o' things before they come to what we read about 'em. 'Master,' says one, 'there's a learned man up to Jerusalem called Nicodemus. He came one night

and had a long talk with Jesus. Shall we go and
ask him what he do think?'

"'Master,' says the other, 'there's our old comrades, John an' Andrew an' Simon. They've been
with Him a good long time now, an' seen His wonders an' heard His words. Shall we go and ask one
o' them? They would come directly I'm sure, and
they'd tell us a great many things about Him.'

"But the poor prisoner didn't look up. He only
shook his head. But we should have jumped at it,
Frankey. We should have said in a minute: 'Iss,
iss—do 'ee go and ask them what they do think.'
Why, there's hundreds o' people go sendin' their
doubts beggin' for scraps to everybody's door, tryin'
to pick up an old dry crust of a proof here, and a
crumb o' comfort there. I've met scores of 'em,
Frankey, an' been one of 'em myself, too, before
now. They'll send their doubts anywhere but the
right place to be rid of 'em. They'll read great big
books 'pon the *Evidences* by any mortal that cares
to write about 'em, every book *except one*, an' that's
the Book o' which our Lord says, *Search the Scrip-
tures. That* they never think of. I fancy that the
old lion began to roar in his cage: 'No, no. Go
right away to Jesus His own self an' ask Him—
John sent us from his prison to ask Thee, Master,
Art Thou He that should come, or do we look for
another?'"

" There, Frankey—that's a bit o' comfort for us,
isn't it ? We *can* send our doubts right away to
Jesus, His own self. What So-and-so says, or what
such-an-one thinks, what good is that ? Tell us Thyself, Master. *Art Thou He that should come, or do*
we look for another ? When He will speak to us I
wonder that we can go wanderin' about listenin' and
arguin' with everybody else about it."

Frankey's lips moved in prayer as Dan'el paused
a moment.

" An' yet I am pretty sure o' one thing, Frankey.
I expect John felt like as if it wasn't a nice kind
o' thing to do, it was like suspectin' his Friend, and
it seemed so cruel for to doubt Him."

Frankey's tender heart caught at the objection
in a moment. With a pained and anxious look
he set his eyes upon Dan'el. " It do, my dear
leader, it do seem cruel to doubt Him.—An' so it
is, too. Go on, my dear leader." And Frankey
waited eagerly for this difficulty to be cleared.

" I don't know if John thought o' what I did,
Frankey. It came to my mind directly. If He is
so lovin' an' humble as to carry my *sins*, I'm quite
sure He won't refuse for to carry my *doubts* too.
' Blessed Jesus,' I said, ' if Thou dost love me so
well as to bear my curse, Thou wilt bear my doubts
too.' "

" Bless Him," cried Frankey as the light broke,

with tears of joy. " O' course, my dear leader,
o' course : so He will, bless Him ; I'm sure He
will."

Again Dan'el turned to the Bible, the trusty
forefinger guiding his eye as he read on :

" *Go and show John again those things which ye do
hear and see.* Look, Frankey, the Blessed Jesus
wasn't angry with him for sendin' his disciples and
askin' that question. Surely that there promise was
meant for poor doubtin' folks : ' If any of you lack
wisdom, let him ask of God, that giveth to all men
liberally, and *upbraideth not.*' He never scolds His
poor, ignorant scholars, though they come askin'
troublesome an' foolish questions that they ought to
have known years ago. Ah, the Blessed Jesus is
the One to send our doubts to ! Why, I shouldn't
wonder but Nicodemus would have said that ' he
was quite surprised, he was, that the Baptist after
preaching to other people should come to be amongst
the doubters his own self.' An' Simon would have
spoke out quite sharp to his old master. An' John,
who hadn't got the blessin' o' perfect love then,
would have flushed up like he did against the
Samaritans. I do know a good many folks to-day,
if you were to send your doubts to them, they'd send
back a message that you ought to be ashamed o'
yourself goin' arguin', an' reasonin', an' doubtin'.
Ah, Frankey, that isn't like the Blessed Lord Jesus.

Seemin' to me as if so soon as ever He got the message He would be sure to think—' Poor, faithful John, thou'rt in the dungeon, cast down an' tempted. I will comfort thee an' strengthen thy faith.' He didn't say, ' Go, tell John to believe.' No; the Blessed Lord gave him something for his faith to take hold of, an' for it to hold on to."

Dan'el turned over the pages of the Bible until he came to the seventh chapter of Luke. He read from the twenty-first verse : "' And in that same hour He cured many of their infirmities and plagues, and of evil spirits ; and unto many that were blind He gave sight. Then Jesus answering said unto them, Go your way, and tell John what things ye have seen and heard.' That is the Blessed One to send our doubts to, Frankey. That same hour He will work a hundred miracles for to hush our fears an' for to gladden our hearts."

The light touched Frankey's face again. " Bless Him," he whispered, " He *is* a gracious and pitiful Saviour—bless Him."

" I wonder what the things were that He said to them," Dan'el went on. " I should dearly like to have been there that day : it must have been very gentle an' comfortin', Frankey—balm for poor John's wounds. I can't help fancyin' that a wonderful tenderness like came over the heart o' Jesus, tender-hearted as He always was. You see He do keep on

talkin' about John for a long time after, an' finishes
it all up with a'most the tenderest words He ever
spoke : *Come unto* ME, *all ye that labour and are
heavy laden, and I will give you rest.*"

" Bless Him," whispered Frankey again.

" Ah, yes, Frankey, thou may'st well bless Him.
He cares for thee every bit so much as for John the
Baptist. Thou ben't no such great man as he was,
Frankey, but mind what Jesus said : *He that is
least in the Kingdom of Heaven is greater than he.*
But I was sayin' that seemin' to me like as if the
thought o' poor John was in the heart of Jesus for
a long time. 'Tis just the same as if He was in-
viting poor, timid folks to come and ask Him all
about the things that do puzzle them. *Learn of
Me*, He says ; *for I am meek and lowly in heart.*
Meek—you see, Frankey, the Blessed Jesus won't
lose His temper because we don't understand the
lesson quicker or learn it better. *Meek and lowly
in heart.* He'll take the infant class, He will, an'
be so patient with the most troublesome of 'em
an' make it all plain to the stupidest. *Ye shall find
rest unto your souls.*"

" 'Tis true, my dear leader, every word, bless
Him. I *do* love Him for it, sure 'nough." And the
glow of his face and the hands clasped again in
rapture told that the tempter had left him, " for a
season " at least.

Dan'el shut up the Bible and rose for prayer with the sick man. Then as if the thought flashed across him, he stayed a moment. "There is one thing more, Frankey, that I meant to say, too. I was thinkin' of it the other day as I was hammerin' away to my work when 'twas dismal an' rainy. *The promises* are just the same 'pon dull days as 'pon fine shiny ones, every bit, and do hold just so good as ever. The Bank o' Heaven isn't broke because the sun is clouded up a bit. Though we do get cast down, and though the devil do hale us off to the dungeon, an' tell us that we shall never get out no more, bless 'ee, Frankey, he's a ould liar, and you can never believe a word he do say."

"He is, my dear leader. I do know that much about 'un."

"Bless 'ee, we *shall* get out again, Frankey. He do know we shall. He can't help the sunshine a-comin' through the iron gratin'; and we cry out like David: 'Hope thou in God: for I shall yet praise Him, Who is the health of my countenance, and my God.' Then seemin' to me like as if the Blessed Lord, Who lets the sighin' o' the prisoner come before Him, do know the voice of His child in there in a minute, and He do knock at the prison door directly, an' do make the old gaoler bring out and deliver the soul that he dared to shut up. 'The Lord looseth the prisoners.'"

"O Lord, thou art my Lord," cried Frankey,
" *my* Lord ! "

"You know, Frankey, when Jesus was born
there was the glory o' the Lord streamin' down and
the heavenly host singin'. 'Twas all light and
music. But very soon the light died out, and the
music died away ; but *the Blessed Jesus was there
still.* And Joseph an' Mary had to get up and go
away out in the dark night, out in the cold winds
an' the bitter rains, to Egypt. But for all it was so
dark and cold, the young Child was in the mother's
arms. An' I expect, Frankey, that every time there
come a very cold blast Mary pressed Him in all the
closer to her heart, an' when she fancied she heard
the soldiers shoutin', she put her arms about Him
more tenderly than ever. Iss, Frankey, the light
an' music may go, *but Jesus won't.* An' the cold
an' dark an' the old enemy, why, they only make
Him nearer an' dearer than ever. 'Tis only when
we do come to the prison or like that, that we know
how good an' how lovin' He is. When we're walkin' about in the garden o' the Lord, He doesn't
speak to us then like He does when we are goin' in
at the dungeon door. Seemin' to me like as if the
Blessed Jesus do come close to us then, and He do
take hold o' our hand, an' all His lovin' heart comes
out in what He do say : ' Fear not, fear not ; I will
never leave thee, I will never forsake thee. Dun-

geon, fire, floods, death, devils, hell, come what may, I will be with thee. An' be quite sure that the more thou dost need ME the more thou shalt have ME. I **will** never leave thee.' "

"Never," cried Frankey rapturously, "never, never, never ! "

III

Frankey Vivian gets out of Doubting Castle, and goes Home.

LMOST at dawn of the next morning Dan'el sat with Frankey again. There was a change that saddened the tone in which he spoke. The features were pinched and shrunk; the breathing was more difficult. As Dan'el stood by him Frankey opened his eyes and looked up, and in a moment the old joy and light shone brighter than ever.

"Well—how is it to-day?" asked Dan'el, shaking the wasted hand tenderly.

"Better an' better, my dear leader," gasped

Frankey. "I've been longin' for 'ee to come that I might tell 'ee about it. Victory! my dear leader, —victory through the blood of the Lamb!" It was with difficulty that he spoke at first, often stopping to get breath, but his body seemed to gather strength from the joyful exulting of his soul, and he went on to tell of his triumph with a wonderful energy:

"He's gone, my dear leader—the old Enemy is gone; clean gone. And I do believe he's gone for ever. Last night I had a terrible bout with un, sure 'nough. Seemin' to me like as if he'd a-gathered up all his strength for to lay me 'pon my back; but bless the Lord, I come off more than conqueror. To think of it, too; why, weak as I am, with my Saviour alongside o' me I'm more than a match for un with all his angels. The words do keep a-ringin' in my ears—I do wish I could sing them once more—: 'Now let my soul arise, And tread the Tempter down.'"

It was Dan'el's voice that took up the words and sang them tenderly to the old familiar 'Trumpet Metre':

> "Now let my soul arise,
>   And tread the Tempter down:
> My Captain leads me forth
>   To conquest and a crown:
> March on, nor fear to win the day,
> Though death and hell obstruct the way."

Frankey tried to go on with the next verse, but
again Dan'el had to take it up and carry it through;
but Frankey's was the rapture that the words
express.

> " Should all the hosts of death,
>   And powers of hell unknown,
>   Put their most dreadful forms
>   Of rage and malice on,
> I shall be safe ; for Christ displays
>   Superior power, and guardian grace."

Then Frankey settled quietly down to tell the story
of his triumph :

"Well, my dear leader, it was last night, all in
the dead o' the night, that I was lyin' here in the
dark when he come 'pon me again and put the
dreadfullest, ghastliest old thoughts in my mind,
you can't think. An' the worst of all was the way
he went on against my Blessed Lord. I can't abide
for to think about them. Then it came into my
mind all in a minute like a flash o' light, yet it came
all so tender an' comfortin' just like as if Jesus His
own self spoke the words to me: *Go and show John
again those things which ye do hear and see.*

"'What dost say, old Tempter?' I called out
aloud. 'The Blessed Lord Jesus Christ doesn't
love me? I'll prove thee a liar. The glorious
Lord will leave me to perish, will He? Bless Him,
I'll show thee something better than that. Come
along with me.' An' I began to think what a won-

derful deal more I had to look at than John the
Baptist ever had.   Blind eyes opened, an' lame
folks walkin', an' lepers cleansed, an' dead men
raised—that's proof enough o' the Blessed Jesus:
but what was all that beside what there was for me
to see ? "

Frankey's voice sank into a great solemnity and
deep tenderness as he went on : " So I took the ould
Tempter up to Gethsemane; up in the shadows o' the
great dark trees.   My own heart was a'most a-break-
in' with love to my Blessed Lord, an' with sorrow
that ever He should have suffered like that.   ' Look
there ! ' I said ; ' cans't thou see that Blessed One
sinkin' there in dreadful agony?   Hark ! canst thou
hear His groans an' cries ?   He is the Son of God,
an' the King of Glory. *An' He's there for me !*   For
me—poor old Frankey Vivian !   Canst thou see the
sweat-drops falling from Him like as if *it were great
drops of blood ?*   For me, all for me ! my blessed,
blessed, Lord !   Ah, look, He falls faintin' 'pon the
ground ! ' "

For a few moments Frankey could not speak.
Then he burst out again triumphantly : " ' Wilt thou
tell me in sight o' *that* that HE doesn't love me ?'

" I turned round, my dear leader, and I did
expect that he'd have gone.   But he didn't stir for
that ; though I couldn't look upon it my own self
without the tears a-streamin' down my cheeks."

"He's a hard-hearted old wretch," put in Dan'el. "But go on, my dear Frankey. I do want to know how you got rid of him."

"'Well,' I says, 'comest along with me again. I will show thee something more than that. To tell me that my Blessed Lord Jesus doesn't love me!' So I took en up to the Judgment Hall."

Again the voice quivered and was broken with emotion. Very slowly, and with his eyes fixed as if on the scene he described, he continued his story:

"'There—canst thou see Him standin' bound at the bar, a poor, forsaken prisoner? There is the well-beloved Son of God! An' He's there for *me!* He's takin' *my* place. Being tried in *my* stead—*mine*, poor old Frankey Vivian! Like as if He had come to me an' said, "Don't you be afraid. I'll go and answer for you." Ah, see how they scourge my Saviour's back! Look — how they pluck the hair off His cheek! They beat Him! They spit upon Him! O, my dear, my glorious Lord, how couldst *Thou* ever love me like that?—*me*, too! How I will praise Thee for it, in a little while!'

"I did think that would have moved the old Tempter, my dear leader. It seemed to me like as if he couldn't say anything in sight of it; but for all that I felt that he was standin' alongside o' me still. I knew I was gettin' the best of it,—bless

my lovin' Lord!—so I spoke out braver than
ever :

"'I haven't done with 'ee yet,' I says out loud;
' come, an' I will show thee something.'"

More slowly and more solemnly still, Frankey
spoke now : " So I took him up the Hill of Calvary.
Ah, what a sight that is, dear leader, isn't it ?
And all for *me !* Why, it do melt my heart for to
think about it.

"'There,' I says, ' thou poor old Tempter, canst
thou see Him now ? Pushed by the crowd ; hooted
at from all sides ; there is *my* Lord, my own Blessed
Jesus ! Dost see that crown of thorns upon His
holy head ? Look ! He staggers under that awful
cross—*For me :* for poor old Frankey Vivian ! And
canst thou see Him hanging on the cross—*for me :*
naked, bleeding, torn, dyin' for my soul ? There—
that is how *He* loves me—He gave Himself for
me !' "

Frankey's voice failed him for a minute or two.
His eyes were fixed as if the scene stood out there
visibly before him.

" My own Blessed Lord ! an' to think that I
could ever have doubted *Thee !* "

Then presently he went on again in a cheery
way, turning his face to Dan'el : " Well, my dear
leader, I looked round to see what the old Tempter
thought o' that—and, bless 'ee, he was gone, clean

gone! I tell 'ee what I think,—I don't believe he
can set foot 'pon Calvary's Hill; so I do mean to
keep right up under the Cross, out of his road if I
can. Bless the Lord, I am right in under there
now, my dear leader; and 'tis wonderful shelter—
a beautiful place, hid in the clefts o' the rock."

Then Frankey sank back exhausted. Dan'el
still held the wasted hand in his own, but his heart
was too full for speech. There was not a sound
except the whispered " Bless Him," " Bless Him,"
that escaped from Frankey's lips.

It was after a long silence that Frankey quietly
finished the story :

'An' that wasn't all, my dear leader. Why, it
was just like when the Blessed Lord Himself was
tempted. The devil left Him, and angels came an'
ministered unto Him. Only He His own self came
to me. I was so quiet an' happy in there under the
shadow of my dear Saviour, that I went to sleep.
I s'pose things got mixed up in my dream, and I
dreamed that I was going along a dreadful dreary
place. There was nothing but a dead tree or two,
an' a lonely moor with a ghastly old pond in the
middle of it, full o' dreadful mockin' things. Tho
grass was all yellow an' dyin', and the sky was all
dull and dismal—it was a wished old place, sure
enough. Well, I thought that I went on a long,
long way, an' I began to think that I should never

see anybody there, when all of a sudden I heard a
voice callin' to me. It spoke so lovin' that I knew
in a moment it was Jesus.

"'Poor lonely wanderer,' He said; 'come over
here to me.'

"I looked up, an' there was the loveliest place
you ever saw. The sun was shinin'; the birds were
singin' beautiful. The trees were some o' them
covered with green leaves, an' some with white
blossom, an' some bendin' down with all sorts o'
delicious fruits. The flowers, too, were everywhere, and I could smell how sweet they were, as I
stood there. Well, I ran so fast as I could to reach
it, an' to see Who was callin' me, for I couldn't see
anybody there, when I came to a little river. It
wasn't very wide, but it was very deep, an' I couldn't
get across.

"Then I heard the voice again, so tender an'
lovin', 'I am waitin' for thee at the bridge. Come
on.'

"I looked where the sound came from, and there
was a little crossin' place. So I hastened to it, and
when I got nearer I heard sweet voices singin'.
Then I saw Jesus directly, just like John saw Him,
—in the white robe, girt with the golden girdle,—
and He beckoned to me.

"'I am comin', my gracious Lord,' I said.

"And then I woke up and found myself here

still in the loneliness an' the dark. But I've had the sweet music a-ringin' in my ears ever since. An' I'm gettin' near to the bridge, my dear leader —nearer an' nearer."

Dan'el could but look on that face lit up with rapturous joy, and think how soon it would shine brighter still with the glory of the Lord; how soon those eyes would behold "the King in His beauty" in the land that to him was *not* "afar off."

He turned over the pages of the Bible until he came to the last chapter of the Revelation; then he read:

"*And he showed me a pure river of water of life, clear as crystal, proceeding out of the throne of God and of the Lamb. In the midst of the street of it, and on either side of the river, was there the tree of life, which bare twelve manner of fruits, and yielded her fruit every month: and the leaves of the tree were for the healing of the nations. And there shall be no more curse: but the throne of God and of the Lamb shall be in it; and His servants shall serve Him: and they shall see His face; and His name shall be in their foreheads. And there shall be no night there; and they need no candle, neither light of the sun; for the Lord God giveth them light: and they shall reign for ever and ever.*"

*   *   *   *   *   *

That night the end came. Frankey's wife and

children were gathered around his bed, while Dan'el sat at his side.

His mind was wandering; his thoughts were in the mine work of former days. His failing breath now made him gasp painfully at the end of almost every word:

" There—comrades—the day's work—is done,— an' I'm—tired out.—I do reckon—that—'tis most time—to go—home long—isn't it ?—I'm goin'—up now.—I shan't light—a fresh candle.—This 'll last —till I do—get up to—to grass."

Then came silence for a few moments.

" Ah—I can mind—once—'twas a Saturday— night.—I was timberman—an' had to—look after everything—when the men—was all gone.—And while—I was goin' along—my candle went out.— A great drop o' water—fell 'pon it.—There I was— all in the dark—and shafts all about—an' the ladder —ever so far off. An' I—hadn't a match.—An' I —kneeled down—an' prayed—an' I asked—the Cap'n—the Lord I mean—to guide me.—An' He did—bless Him !—Led me—along—by the hand— —till I got hold o' the ladder.—But now—bless the Lord—the candle is burnin'.—" An' ye yourselves —like unto men—that wait for—their Lord,—when He will return from—the weddin'.' "

Then came a longer silence, and his breathing grew more difficult.

"Aw—it do—take away—all my breath—goiu' up—the ladder. I shan't be sorry—when—I've had —my last climb—an' done—with it. But there—the last climb—of all—won't be—so hard—either. 'Run up—with joy—the shiniu' way—To see—an' praise —my Lord.' Yes—*my* Lord—my own blessed,— blessed Lord.—Come—let's stop—a bit an' sing once more: 'Come—let us join—our cheerful songs.'"

Then Frankey lay as if listening with rapture to some singing that none else heard. Now and then he lifted his hand as if in time with it, and faintly whispered, "'Tis lovely, lovely."

Dan'el could not help thinking of that sweet music of which Frankey had spoken, that came not from earth, but from the garden of the Lord.

"My blessed, blessed Jesus," Frankey cried with sudden energy, "Why, 'tis—Heaven—sure 'nough— to hear—Thy dear name—praised—like that.—But now—come on—comrades—come on—We're goin' home—goin' home. They're—lookin' out—for me— I know. An' then—supper—an' rest—rest.—'Tis hard work—now—but *then* rest—rest—Ye shall— find—rest to your—souls."

Again silence; so sudden and complete that Dan'el leaned forward thinking Frankey was gone. But presently the voice broke out again, with more firmness and strength:

"There—I can breathe—better now.—I'm up

at last.—Yes—out with the candle—blow it out.—
We shan't want—that—any more.—They need—no
candle—nor light—o' the sun.—Bless the Lord!

"And now—into the changin' room—for to put
off—my workin' clothes.' A smile played over the
face for a moment. 'This mortal—must put on—
immortality—an' then—home. Home an' rest—
an' supper.—Sit down with Him—to the Marriage
Supper—That's right—sing, my dear comrades—
beautiful!—beautiful!"

Again there was a short silence, then Frankey
turned his eyes around the room and smiled on them
all, and seemed as if he were going to speak to them
by name; but suddenly he looked upward fixedly,
whilst a wonderful joy lit his face.

"They're comin'," he whispered, "comin'."
Keeping his eyes gazing on the same place, he cried
aloud—"What, these for me!—for me!—white
robes!—an' angels—to wait 'pon me!—My Blessed
Lord—'tis like Thee—'zactly—as if Thou—canst
never do—enough for me.—There—I'm ready now
—waitin'—O, my blessed, blessed——'!

Then suddenly Frankey was gone.

IV

Dan'el's trouble, and What he Did with it.

ATTERS had not been in a very flourishing state for some time past in the little Church at Penwinnin.

To Dan'el this was the most sorrowful of all things that could happen. Business might fall off: it often did, for there were long and grievous times of depression in mining, when the men had to emigrate, and wives and children were sorely pinched; then the long bills at the shoemaker's could not be paid, and Dan'el's store of savings went in helping the needy ones about him. But at such times it was a real treat to meet him. You were sure to find scores of dismal croakers predicting, in awful tones, the ruin of the whole county, if not of England itself : what with America or Australia or some other place, they could never look up again ; so they declared.   And they spoke it so solemnly, and so stubbornly, that it never occurred to you to doubt it for a moment. Then you came into the shoemaker's little shop, and Dan'el's face looked from his work as cheerily as ever.   You began, naturally enough, to repeat these doleful opinions.   As he listened the lips were tightened ; the round head was vigorously nodded. There came a pause of a minute, as if he were try-ing to hold back the indignation that was gathering within him.   Then suddenly it burst out, as if it could not be restrained :

" Aw, 'tis dreadful, dreadful.   That folks can go talkin' such nonsense !   An' all because they haven't had the makin' o' the world their own selves.   How pretty they would ha' made it, wouldn't they ?   Why, Carn Brea would ha' been a great mountain o' pure gold, an' Beacon Hill too.   An' pretty lots o' fightin' an' stealin' an' murderin' we should have had 'long with it, shouldn't we ?

" Why, I don't believe that there ever was a country that went to ruin for want o' money.   'Tisn't want that ruins 'em ; 'tis this here : Folks get listenin' to the devil : ' I've got the kingdoms o' the world an' the glory of 'em—fall down an' worship me.' An' they sell theirselves to him an' his ways. An' what else can you expect but that he should come an' carry 'em away, body an' soul? Only let folks serve God, an' put their trust in Him, an' they'll go on right enough; with a few ups an' downs, I dare say, just to remind 'em that this is not their restin'-place. An' more than that, I believe you'll find 'em a rich people, too. The silver is Mine, an' the gold is Mine, saith the Lord of Hosts. Of course, the tin is His, an' the copper too. But it doesn't say so—like as if the silver an' the gold was the Lord's in partic'lar. An', depend 'pon it, that He will give that country the most of it that'll do the best with it—that's my belief. I can't abide to hear folks go talkin' like as if our Heavenly Father had nothing to do with us except to save our souls, and to take us out o' this here dreadful world so soon as ever He can. 'Tis *His* world, and His Love an' Wisdom have every bit so much to do with tin an' copper as with anything else. When He hid that away in the rocks, He said " very good " o' that too —an' so 'tis. Why, look how 'tis when we do get a bit prosperous—we do begin to swarm till there's no elbow-room for anybody. Folks are all in each other's road. If we went on like that for long we should be a'most shovin' each other over cliff! An' all the time there's that great Australia over there; so the Father in Heaven do let them find a bit o'

gold or a bunch o' tin, and off goes scores an' hundreds o' young chaps, an' we home here do get a
bit o' breathin' room again, an' very soon things
come to be so good as ever.   Why, to hear folks
grumble an' growl as they do, you'd reckon that
things was put together a-purpose to spite 'em, instead o' believin' with David that *the earth is full
o' the goodness o' the Lord.*"

Then Dan'el caught up the half-made boot, and
stitched away at it fiercely, tugging at the threads
as if they somehow clenched the argument.

Plainly enough the time to find Dan'el cast down
was not when the tall chimney stacks stood smoke-
less and the engines idle; when the roar of the
stamps had ceased, and there was no clanking of the
chains; when the piles of stones lay heaped up in
desolate confusion, and the " dressing-floors " were
no longer crowded with the busy groups of boys
and girls.

But let things droop in the Church, and Dan'el
was a changed man.   When the Word was preached
without the manifest power of the Spirit; yet more,
when strife and bitterness sprang up amongst the
people—*that* took all heart out of him.   Many times
a day the work would be laid down, and as the eye
looked vacantly out of the window a great sigh
would come from his troubled soul.   Frequently the
little place was left for half-an-hour whilst Dan'el

went away alone with God, pouring out his heart in
earnest pleading.   And half the night long he lay
sleepless at such times, thinking and sorrowing and
praying.

The chief cause of Dan'el's grief just now was
John Trundle, the village shopkeeper.   John had
been for years a dead weight upon the little Church
at Penwinnin; now he somewhat suddenly became
a living obstruction and plague.   The fickle Wheal
Gambler, that had worn out the patience and pockets
of hundreds, had at last "cut rich" as they said.
Trundle, living on the spot and getting hints of the
more kindly appearance of things, had bought up
all the shares that he could, and now leapt into a fortune.   It was all so sudden, and so much, that it completely turned his head, and his heart too.   Nothing
was good enough now for a man of so much importance.   The little chapel in which he had wor-
shipped all his days, where hundreds of saints had
found the wedding garment and gone "triumphant
home," was a poor and despised place.   He really
couldn't ask his friends inside those mean, white-
washed walls; so he had to go off to the parish
church, where he found himself sadly inconvenienced
by the order of the service, and turned his brand-
new Prayer-Book almost inside out—as well as he
could with his tightly-buttoned gloves—in search
of the Psalms and the Collect for the day.

Some of the Preachers, simple-hearted, godly men, upon whose efforts the Most High had set the broad seal of His sanction, were almost openly sneered at as men not fit to hold forth in the presence of Mr. John Trundle and his family; and even Dan'el himself was criticized as "really very rough and unpolished."

Now whilst nothing could have made this any other than a contemptible impertinence, there were some things that might perhaps have made it a little more reasonable. For instance, if Mr. John Trundle had been willing to pay for the indulgence of his whims: if, as he had paid for a larger house and a grander style of life, he had been willing to pay for a nobler place of worship and for daintier services, there would have been at least a consistency in his proceedings. But this was by no means the course that Mr. John Trundle adopted: indeed, it was precisely the reverse of this. He had become at once more exacting and more miserly, more demanding and yet more niggardly. He had always given little enough; now he gave no more, but felt himself entitled to give it with a grumble; indeed, as he increased in importance, he gave it with a threat that he certainly should not continue to contribute unless, etc., etc. So this man, who had never been a very bright or shining light in the little Church at Penwinnin, let the flickering flame of his religion go quite out; but the wick still went on smouldering with an offensive " smeach " that annoyed almost everybody, and that roused all Daniel's righteous indignation.

It might have been more endurable if the evil had been confined to Trundle himself. As a rich man, however, one upon whom Providence had smiled so brightly, there were some always ready to side with him—to echo what he said without a doubt and with a boisterous emphasis. Moreover, half-a-dozen disaffected grumblers like old Widow Pascoe, to whom complaining and gloomy murmuring were the truest signs of grace—did it not prove that the earth to them was a howling wilderness? —rejoiced with almost questionable delight to find so influential a leader as this.

Such was the state of things as Dan'el sat one day thinking of his Class that was to meet in the evening. For a week past the sacred old Bible, in its green baize covers, had been set up before him as he worked, opened day after day at the thirteenth and fourteenth of Genesis, until Dan'el must have known the verses by heart. As the sharp little eye turned to the page, or when it was lifted from the work for a moment, as some thought flashed upon him, there was a strange fierceness in it. Then, too, Dan'el hammered at the leather with a sharp, half-angry hammering; he thrust in the brad-awl with an energetic jerk; he caught at the wax-end with a tighter grip.

But at noon of this day the fierceness failed him. His grief, the thought of his own helplessness, his longing that the glory of the Lord should appear amongst them again, overcame him. The dinner lay before him untasted. His hands hung down idly by his side as he leaned back in the chair, and tears crept down his rugged cheeks. At length he roused himself: he could not go on like this. The fierceness came back in the energy with which he flung on his coat and his hat, and turned the key in the door. Then leaving word with the neighbour that he should not be back until evening, Dan'el started off at a vigorous pace that soon left Penwinnin behind.

It was in the early spring, and there was a tender balminess in the air as if in pity for all the young life that was just coming into being after a long and dreary winter. His way led down the rugged, winding hill-path; then under a long row of elms, their dainty young leaves playing shyly with the gentle breeze; on through the fields, all snowy white with daisies, except in the marshy slope where the golden "lent lilies" nodded on their slender stems. Then along by the red mill-stream that went racing eagerly, as if it heard the clatter and splash of the wheel and loved the sport of sending it creaking round; over little rivulets that came oozing out from the bank, as if their courage failed them and they were creeping timidly away from that long leap into the darkness. Past the little house, its thatched roof a very garden of moss and "penny-pies" and house-leek, of haughty "London Pride," and aspiring groundsel; then round by the mill itself, the whitened half-door shut, and the darkness above it presently relieved by the miller, as he came out with a friendly nod, glad to have the loneliness broken by a passer by. Round by the dripping wheel, the wet walls thick with clusters of ferns; across the muddy red river, going deep and silent to the solemn sea; up a steep bit of hill—and then Dan'el stops to breathe the fresh sea-breeze that greets him.

Already the kindly hand of Nature is charming the sorrow out of his face, and the grief out of his vexed heart. Away before him and on either hand stretches the heather, and the golden furze, lading the air with its fragrance, whilst from the cloudless sky the lark pours constantly a flood of rapturous music. The old brightness comes back again when, a little distance farther, Dan'el catches sight of the far-off sea line. Then only a few steps more, and there burst upon him the view that always filled his soul with joy.

Below, for three hundred feet, there stretched

the rugged cliff; here, broken, heaped up stones; there, patches of dark green grass and purple heather; then steep crags and shady hollows; and elsewhere the smooth steep bit that some landslip had swept sheer down to the black rocks below. Out at sea, there were the long lines in which the waves were curving; sweeping on for a while unbroken, then lifting up white crested heads, and coming on arched and majestic, to be dashed into showers of spray, or breaking on the beach, where they went creeping far up the sands, white-lipped and harmless. And away beyond all this, "rounding it off with infinity," stretched the Atlantic, transparent green where the yellow sand lay underneath it, merging on either side into the deepest blue. Far up and down the coast projecting headlands, bold and rugged, shut in the view. The only sounds were the ringing music of the lark and the deep bass of the sea. A score of gulls that went sailing overhead with scarce a beat of their white wings, and a lonely "shag" that flew heavily along the water, completed the scene.

Dan'el stood for some minutes wrapt in delicious enjoyment, drinking in its beauty. Suddenly his face grew clouded, as if some stray thought from Penwinnin had followed its master and found him.

" 'Tis a wonder," he muttered, "a wonder, sure 'nough !" And he confirmed the opinion by sighing

deeply and slowly nodding his head. " 'Tis a wonder—that with such a lovely world for Himself, the
Blessed Lord should put up with us troublesome
men and women! 'Tis a wonder!" And again
Dan'el looked forth upon it all: the sky, the cliff,
the sea. Then his voice was softened as he said:
" My kind, my loving Lord! It *do* hurt me for to
think of it—that Thou should have made all this for
us, and that we should give Thee back nothin' but
grief an' grumblin' ! "

It really seemed that fair Nature had failed as
a comforter after all, as Dan'el stood there repeating
the words—"nothin' but grief an' grumblin' ! "
But the beauty of the scene got the best of it again
presently. Dan'el shook himself as if flinging off all
his load: " But come, Dan'el; thou art here alone
with thy Heavenly Father, an' thou must find a
sweeter offering for Him than sighs an' groans. I
will too, my Blessed Lord—for I *do* love Thee for
makin' things so beautiful." And he hurried down
the steep little path singing cheerily as he went:

> " Eternal Wisdom! Thee we praise,
>   Thee the creation sings ;
> With Thy loved name, rocks, hills, and seas,
>   And Heaven's high Palace rings."

So down the long descent until he reached the
sandy beach. Then across the little bay—where
the deep solitude was very seldom broken by any

intruder; and there amongst the rocks was Daniel's
Temple; a place to which he had come many times
before to plead with God, when he wanted, as he
said, " to get right away alone with the Lord for
something particular." It was a cave, not deep but
high and rounded. The floor was of the whitest
sand, decked here and there with a spray of sea-
weed. The walls shining with the moisture, looked
like polished pillars. The roof was fretted into
curious pendants and projections, and strangely
dyed, for a copper vein ran in the rock, and this
acted upon by the salt water had stained the roof
with brilliant blues and greens of exquisite beauty.

Dan'el stood for a moment, in the low arched
entrance, looking out upon the scene—the towering
cliffs and tossing sea. " 'Tis just like Elijah," he
murmured to himself, " when he turned aside and
lodged in a cave. An' there—dear old Frankey is
gone, and I'm a'most ready to say, ' I, even I only,
am left. . . . Take away my life; for I am not
better than my fathers.' " Like Elijah he had been
certainly in the earlier part of that memorable day—
fierce, indignant, jealous for the Lord of Hosts, yet
depressed and wearied at heart. But now, hid here
in the clefts of the rock, it was like Moses that
Dan'el pleaded with God on behalf of the Church at
Penwinnin. He took upon his heart their sins and
carried them with his own as a great burden before

the Lord. He took hold of the precious promises
and pleaded them. He entreated the Most High for
His own Name's sake. Nor did he ask in vain—
such earnest pleading cannot fail. To him, as to
Moses in the old time, the Lord came near and pro-
claimed Himself, and made His goodness to pass
before his servant. And like Moses, too, Dan'el
gathered up the souls of whom he had the care, and
cried concerning them: "O Lord, let my Lord, I
pray Thee, go among us; for it is a stiff-necked
people; and pardon our iniquity and our sin, and
take us for Thine inheritance."

  *   *   *   *   *   *

It was with quite another look that Dan'el turned
as he reached the top of the cliff again some two
hours afterward, to rest a bit after his steep climb
and to get a last sight of the sea. The sunshine
fell full upon his face and seemed to light it up with
hope and joy. There was no fierceness now; no
fretting trouble. All was peace: a restful and assured confidence that all should yet be well. And
turning towards home he stepped out with a buoy-
ancy and firmness, as of one who had waited on the
Lord and *renewed his strength,* and so could *run, and
not be weary,* could walk all the days of life and not
faint.

"There," said Dan'el, as he reached home and
set the stout walking-stick behind the door of tho

little cottage. " There; that's what I do a'most call a cure-all—a six mile walk, a view like that, and a good time with my Blessed Master is real good physic sure 'nough, for body, soul, an 'spirit.   And 'tis a brave deal nicer than doctor's trade, too."

V

Dan'el's Trouble, and What he Said about it.

 ROTHER DAN'EL was ready for the meeting now. As he took his place that evening in the sanded front kitchen at Thomas Toms', there was all the vigour, the joy, the sprightliness that had drooped for some weeks. He gave out the hymn with a ringing triumph, as if his soul were making its boast in the Lord:

"God is the Refuge of His saints,
  When storms of sharp distress invade;

Ere we can offer our complaints,
Behold Him present with His aid!"

Dan'el might have been lying still in the pleasant and hallowed shelter of the cave, listening to the dash of the waves outside, he so "entered into" the words of the third verse :

" Loud may the troubled ocean roar ;
In sacred peace our souls abide ;
While every nation, every shore,
Trembles, and dreads the swelling tide."

And the next verse came with such tenderness, and such manifest relish on the leader's part, that even Widow Pascoe was stirred into looking at the words to see what it was that she had never noticed in them before :

" There is a Stream, whose gentle flow
Supplies the city of our God ;
Life, love, and joy still gliding through,
And watering our divine abode."

Then in the fulness and power of the afternoon's blessing, Dan'el drew near to the Throne of Grace, leading the little company into the very presence of God, and inspiring them with his own boldness.

Dan'el had but one rule in the order of his Class-meeting. Whatever the Class-meeting is or is not, it surely was never meant to be a round of vague little sermons ; still less was it meant to be for preaching the very same little sermons, week after

week, until everybody knows them "by heart."
Heart-talk — real, fresh, living heart-talk — this
Dan'el must have, and would. Almost anything
that kept away a dead sameness, in form or phrase,
commended itself to him at once. So Dan'el had no
difficulty in bringing in the result of the week's
meditation. He began at once :

"Friends, I've been thinkin' that I can't do
better to-night than talk a bit from *the Word*. My
mind has been runnin' a good deal lately 'pon this
story here, in the thirteenth chapter of Genesis. An'
I may so well give 'ee some o' my thoughts about
it while they are warm."

Just then a late comer lifted the latch of the
door with much clatter, and was bustling at the mat
outside. Dan'el waited, for all eyes were turned
from him.

"I've heard 'em say that when poverty knock to
the door, love do fly out through the window. Well,
that may be true, or it mayn't. But this here is
always true : when late comers do open the door,
listenin' do fly out o' the window, or up the chimney,
or somewhere. 'Tis all gone."

Just as the sentence was finished, John Trundle
appeared at the open door. He was always late—in
the old time because the village shop demanded his
presence. "*Business must be attended to,*" was a
great saying, which he quoted as solemnly as if it

were in the Bible; and on the strength of its warrant
the Prayer-meeting, the Class-meeting, and every
other week-night service must stand aside. Now
that he was not so dependent on the village shop,
he was always late still; perhaps because he did
not care enough about the meeting to come in time;
possibly, too, because it added to the sense of his
own importance. A man of such influence was not
going to be told when he should come.

Dan'el waited a little longer, until the disturb-
ance had ceased and Trundle had found a chair;
then he went on again very good-humouredly :

" Glad to see 'ee, John; though, there, I would
rather have had 'ee here in time to begin, too.
'Twas a lovely hymn that we had. But just as you
came in I was sayin' that we would have a talk
from the Word to-night. 'Tis in the thirteenth
chapter o' Genesis—about Lot. Now I'm fine an'
sorry that 'tis a subject we do want so much up
here to Penwinnin. But seein' that 'tis, well—I've
picked it out on purpose, for I'm bound to try an'
find the physic that will do most good. 'Tisn't
kind, nor right neither, to go givin' folks sweet-
meats and gingerbreads when they'm bad for want
o' bitters; to be a-poulticin' of 'em with figs when
they be dyin' for want of a blister. So here is a
subject for us to think about, an' the Lord help
every one of us to take out of it what'll do us good."

Dan'el spoke with a yearning tenderness that went to every heart. The thoughts that had been caught at so fiercely during the week; that had been stitched and hammered at so vigorously, came out now, not softened or edgeless, but with an intense desire for the good of his little flock that all felt and most of them at once responded to.

"We'll begin here to the fifth verse," Dan'el went on; the stout forefinger guiding his sharp eye to the words : "*And Lot which went with Abram.*— There, I don't want for to say anything unkind about the man, but I can't help thinkin' somehow as if that there was the secret of it all. Depend 'pon it, that's how it was that Lot could ever come to settle in that dreadful city—he only *went with Abram.* He hadn't heard the Voice of God callin' him to the land o' Promise; if he had, he never would have gone to Sodom; or when he got there, he would have come out again a brave deal faster than he went in. That's it. He just went 'long with Abram, an' so when he sees a place where he thought he could make his fortune a bit quicker, away he goes, never mind about anything else. 'Tis just the same now-a-days. Lots o' folks think that they are quite religious enough just because they do go along with religious people and call theirselves by the same name. That'll do for a time perhaps. But there, even while it *do* last, they

go along so dull an' heavy that you can see in a
minute their hearts are'nt in it. 'Tisn't a morsel
o' good—not a morsel. I've heard these kind o'
people singin': '*Nail* my affections to the Cross.'
Nail 'em! Why, bless 'ee, they aren't sticked with
so much as a wafer. The first bit o' pleasure that
beckons to 'em, an' they're off: jingle a few pieces
o' silver in their ears an' you can draw 'em anywhere. Friends, let us look right into our hearts
an' make sure that 'tis all right with us. We shall
never reach the Celestial City by just goin' along
with good folks that are 'pon the road. A man
must have the Voice of God comin' right home to
his own heart an' callin' him into the land that He
will show us. Why, once when Jesus was goin'
across the sea, it do say that there was a lot o' little
ships that *went with Him.* But when the storm
came they wanted something more than that: they
wanted the Blessed Master *aboard* with 'em then.
'Twas only them that were in the ship with Him
that could come an' say, 'Master, carest Thou not
that we perish?' Goin' along with the Lord Jesus
Himself wasn't enough. So soon as ever it began
to blow a bit the little ships ran for the harbour;
an' before that I expect some of 'em drifted away
with the current; an' some saw a big fish an' got
the lines overboard; and by the time the Lord was
to the other side you don't hear anything more

R

about them. We must have the Lord Jesus aboard with us, friends. It must be Christ in the heart; or we shall part company with Him, like Lot did with Abraham.

"But there is another thing that we mustn't forget. *And Lot also, which went* **with Abram, had** *flocks, and herds, and tents.*—There, friends, let us mind that. 'Tisn't salvation to go 'long with good people, but mind you 'tis *a good thing for all that.* So long as Lot went with Abram he had flocks, an' herds, an' tents. But when he left Abram he lost all he had, and lost it all twice over. Goin' with good folks is a good thing. You're a'most sure to pick up some o' the heavenly manna that the Blessed Father do send down for His children; for when He opens the windows o' heaven He always sends more than there's room enough to receive, an' then there's a chance for empty souls. Why, I very often see folks so poor an' lean' an' empty in their souls that they can't do nothin' but grumble. Ah! if they'd only get in with some old saint, and have a talk, an' a bit o' prayer, why, they'd pick up so fast that you'd hardly know 'em. There's folks that do call theirselves religious, an' yet they scarce get so much as a crumb o' comfort or a crust o' grace week in or week out."

Dan'el turned significantly to the page of his Class-book, and traced the names of one or two who were frequently absent. He sighed and shook his head.

"Ah, if they'd only fall in with God's people and go 'long with 'em a bit, there'd be a blessin' for 'em very often. 'Tisn't savin', but a man does stand a better chance o' hearin' the Voice of the Lord callin' him if he do keep company with them that are hearin' it all day long. If the little ships hadn't got Jesus aboard, still they shared in the calm when they went with them that could wake Jesus up. 'Twasn't enough to go along with Jesus when He went into the wilderness, but for all that 'twas a good thing—*they did all eat, and were filled.*"

Dan'el stayed a few moments, as if he wanted that to sink in and get settled before he went on again. Then he turned to the open Bible once more.

"*And the land was not able to bear them, . . . for their substance was great, so that they could not dwell together.* Ah! people do think that riches is always good—the best of all good. But here it is doin' what Solomon says o' the talebearer, 'tis separatin' very friends. That was more than famine could do, and all their wanderin's too. 'Tis just the same with a good many folks now-a-days. Let 'em get rich, and there—'tis very soon off with the old love then! 'Twas when *money* knocked to the door that Lot's love flew out o' the window, and 'tis very often like that. And a good thing if their money don't come in between them an' their Best Friend, the lovin' Lord Jesus Himself. But mind, 'tisn't always so. Here's Abraham — he's very rich too, but for all that he isn't altered a bit; just so generous an' friendly as ever. But in a general way, it'll take a man with so much religion an' so big a soul as Abraham had, for to manage it right. I wonder if there's anybody that do ever pray to the Lord like Agur did, that they mayn't get rich."

John Trundle started at the thought and looked up amazed. Could there be any such madness anywhere? And who was Agur? It must be in the Apocrypha: there were all sorts of strange things there; so John had heard.

"Yet many men might do worse things than that. I've heard say that everybody thinks he could drive a gig or manage a small farm. That may be, but I do know that everybody thinks he could do a lot o' good if he only had a lot o' money. I do, my own self—fine an' often. Yet I expect that five out of six of us would go hurtin' ourselves with it, body, soul, an' spirit—an' hurtin' other people too.

"*And there was a strife.*—Iss—there 'tis, you see. I've seen it just the same up here to Penwinniu half-a-dozen times. A sort o' religious man do get rich—then he begins for to think great things of his own self, an' very little things o' everybody else. He begins to go up an' down, scoldin' an' fault-findin'; an stingy too. An' they that are about en do catch his tone, an' do imitate his ways —and so there's sure to be strife in the Church and in the world."

John Trundle coughed timidly as a kind of anxious protest that the cap did not fit him in any degree, and that he did not trace any possible re- semblance to himself.

"I saw a picture once of a young woman, or angel, or something o' that sort, and she had a great horn in her hand filled with all kinds o' flowers an' fruits that she was flingin' out as she went along. The road behind her was all crowded with hungry folks bein' fed, an' ragged folks clothed, an' children bein' learned, and mission- aries preachin'. And on before her all sorts o' horrible things was hurryin' out of her way so fast as ever they could. Underneath the picture there was the young woman's name, an' it was called *Prosperity*. Well, she may be like that sometimes, an' I don't see why she shouldn't be like that always. But she isn't—she isn't. I've a-seen her like an old hag of a witch; with a dreadful evil eye, ill-wishin' everybody; goin' about a-mumblin' an' a-mutterin' all sorts o' things; her hooked

fingers tryin' to claw hold o' everything they come
across. That's more like *Miss Prosperity* very often.
Goin' about partin' friends, an' sowin' strife an'
misery, an' a-grippin' an' a-grindin' everything for
to bake a bigger cake for her own self. Makin'
folks so grand that you don't hardly know 'em, an'
makin' them so high an' mighty that they don't
know you either."

Again Dan'el turned to the chapter.

"Then, friends, I been thinkin' a good deal
about what it do say here: *The Canaanite and the
Perizzite dwelled then in the land.*—Seemin' to me
that this is put in for to show the danger o' the
quarrel. While they was squabblin' with each
other, these here heathens might come and carry
away their flocks an' herds, an' perhaps theirselves
too. I know that 'tis so along with the Church:
only let them begin to quarrel, and the Devil can
steal a'most all they've got. Why, when I was only
a little lad I was old enough for to know that it
was no good goin' fishin' in the still clear water—
they could see 'e in a minute; 'twas in the stickles
an' the broken water that we pulled 'em out. The
Devil can't catch much where 'tis all calm an' peace-
ful. But there—it *do* fret me for to think o' what
the old Enemy have stole from up here lately. 'Tis
dreadful to think about—dreadful! Not to say
nothing about the times he've drove me from my

work, an' the nights that he've stole sleep from my
eyes;—if that was all, why, I could thank en for it,
for he have overshot the mark very often, an' many
an' many a blessin' I've had lately when he've
sent me up to the Throne o' Grace. But there—
only to think what charity the old thief have took
away from us; and what peace o' mind; an' what
zeal for the Lord's work. Why, the very singin'
isn't what it used to be; an' as to power in prayer,
there's scarce any left. An' then, the old thief—
'tisn't only what he do steal. I s'pose he've heard
folks say, 'Exchange is no robbery'—or perhaps
he taught 'em to say so, very likely. So he've left
a lot o' his ghastly old jealousy an' bitterness behind en instead."

As Daniel caught sight of the next verse there
came a longer pause. He sighed deeply, and his
voice sank into its saddest tone.

"That's bad enough; isn't it, friends? But that
isn't all. Listen to this here: *And Abram said unto
Lot, Let there be no strife, I pray thee, between me
and thee.*—Ah! that's the most dreadful thing about
it: ME *and thee.* The words do keep ringin' in my
ears day and night—' ME *and thee.*' "

His voice grew husky, and the tears crept down
his cheeks.

"Think of it, friends. Quarrellin' among the
servants do come to be fightin' against our Blessed

Master. Lot comes up expectin' to meet the angry
blusterin' herdmen, an' he's thinkin' o' the mighty
things he'll say and do. But instead o' that, here
was Abraham comin' to meet him. Why, Abraham
had given Lot everything that he had. He had
taken him up when he was a poor orphan an' been
a father to him. Why, Abraham loved him so well
that he was ready to go out an' risk his life for him,
an' he did too only a little bit later. An' now he
comes up all so grieved-lookin', an' he holds out his
hands an' says: 'Let there be no strife, I pray
thee, between me and thee.' Ah! friends, isn't it
just like the Blessed Lord Jesus do come to you an'
me? He has given us all that we've got: life an'
salvation. 'Tis all o' His mercy that we are out of
hell. He took us into His family and made us His
own children. Ah! bless His holy Name, He has
redeemed our lives from destruction with His precious blood, an' laid down His life for us. An' now,
friends, seemin' to me as if this Blessed Jesus do
come to you an' me to-night, holdin' out His hands
—His pierced hands—an' sayin' all so grieved, *Let
there be no strife, I pray thee, between* ME *and thee*—
ME *and thee*."

For a moment Dan'el's deep feeling overcame
him. Then, as if that Sacred Presence stood there
visibly before him, he bowed his head. "O! my
Blessed Master, I kiss Thy out-stretched hand.

Let me die before ever I should come to be at
strife with Thee, my blessed, crucified Redeemer!"
Presently he looked up, his voice softened and subdued : " Friends, I will take my share to myself, the
Lord helpin' me.   I do know that I'm impatient
very often, an' I do speak out sharp an' quick very
often.   But these here words have come right home
to my heart and a'most broke it : to think that ever
I could be at strife with my loving Saviour !   I've
been away alone with Him to-day, and I've prayed
to Him with all my heart that He would pluck out
this tongue o' mine, and that He'd cut off this
here hand, before ever they should come to quarrel
with Him."

Dan'el covered his face with his hands for a
minute or two, and many another head was bent in
earnest silent prayer.   When he looked up, his face
was bright again and his voice had recovered its
cheery firmness.   "There," said he, wiping his eyes,
" the Lord send that right into our hearts, friends,
and make it stick there for to keep 'em tender.
Amen."

" Amen," responded a score of fervent hearts.

" Well, I don't want to have all the talk to myself; so now, friends, 'tis your turn."   But as Dan'el
spoke he eyed the chapter, and held the cover of
the Book in his hand as if very reluctant to shut it.
" Though there—one *might* say a brave deal more

about it, too—and—' he hesitated and looked round the little room—'if you do think that 'tis so well for me to go on while 'tis all fresh 'pon my mind, I will."

It was young Captain Joe that spoke out: " I believe the Lord gave you the message a-purpose for us, my dear leader ; and if He have, then you're bound to deliver it all."

Almost every head nodded its approbation. Only John Trundle looked as if he wished to break the thread of the discourse ; but he checked himself, and tried to cough a little cough of utter indifference, as if it were a matter that really did not concern him in any way. Widow Pascoe, for her part, maintained an air of severe neutrality.

In a moment the cover of the sacred old Bible dropped back again on the table, and Dan'el's finger lighted at once on the ninth verse.

" *Is not the whole land before thee ?* that's what Abraham said—*separate thyself, I pray thee, from me : if thou wilt take the left hand, then I will go to the right ; or if thou depart to the right hand, then I will go to the left.*—If it be possible, as much as lieth in us, we are to live peaceably with all men. But if you can't, then better part in peace than live in strife. Well, Lot jumps at the chance directly. He was the youngest, and owed everything to Abraham. Never mind that—he was too rich to be generous.

I can hear him mutterin' to hisself: 'A man with so many flocks and herds dependin' upon him must look sharp and take care—'tis a very responsible position.' And I can hear him sayin', too, just like these worldly kind o' religious people go excusin' theirselves to-day: 'You see, uncle is so open-hearted and unsuspectin', that if I didn't take advantage of his kindness, somebody else would—so I s'pose that I must take my choice.' It was bad enough that Lot should choose at all, friends, but 'twas a hundred times worse that he should choose what he did. But let us read about it:

"*He lifted up his eyes.*—There—he walked by sight. An' what he saw was all lovely; a valley well watered everywhere, so beautiful as the garden o' the Lord. Ah! but what he *didn't* see was a good deal more than what he did. It always is. He should have had a bit o' prayer about it; then the Lord would have opened his eyes to see the fires o' hell creepin' up ready to burst upon the place an' to burn 'em all—flocks an' tents an' herds an' everything. Lot saw that the place was well watered everywhere—that was enough, what more could anybody wish for? So away he went, to live there.

"I've got an old book home, and it do say that there was a heavy mortgage on that estate. There was, friends, sure 'nough. Listen to this here in the thirteenth verse: *But the men of Sodom were wicked and sinners before the Lord exceedingly.*—Ah! Lot, if you could get that there estate in a gift, you'd never make anything out of it. So sure as ever you do set foot in the place you'll lose all you've got—an' a nice miss if you don't perish your own self, too.

"I do often see it, friends, fine an' often. And I've watched it for years. Here's a young fellow doin' good in the Sunday-school and other ways, promisin' to be a useful man when we old folks are gone home. You'll hear en singin' so lusty :

> ' Were the whole realm of nature mine,
>   That were a present far too small ;
> Love so amazing, so divine,
>   Demands my soul, my life, my all.'

But somebody sends down word that he can make half-a-crown a week more wages up to London. That's enough. No prayer about it ; no askin' the Lord what He do see. No thinkin' about the Lord's work. He do lift up his eyes and see that 'tis 'well watered,' and he's off. 'I must get on,' says he ; and he says it so pious as if it was one o' the ten commandments—but 'tisn't, friends, 'tisn't, though you do hear it so often. An' I don't believe that there's any *must* about it either. If a man is the Lord's man then I know another *must* that ought to swallow up all the rest, like Aaron's rod swallowed the others : '*I must get up,*' that's the Christian's must, 'an' if I can get on, too, I will. But I *must* get up.'

"There's lot's o' these here Lots about still. Aw iss—iss. 'Tis a nice farm, well watered, an' all that, an' so fine a wheat-growin' parish as there is in the kingdom. But mind the mortgage. 'Tis miles away from any Gospel preachin'; an' you must go where your landlord do; an' you must vote accordin' to his orders. Why, it do put a bit o' temper into me for to see a man o' the world that God have made in His own image an' likeness, go a-sellin' hisself like that. But when 'tis a man that do talk pious about the Lord bein' his Master, an' yet he will go an' sell hisself, body, soul an' spirit, for a bit o' gain, or a bit more business, or a bit o' some fine body's favour, 'tis dreadful sure 'nough! I don't wonder that the Heavenly Father do make 'em smart for it, like He did Lot. An' serve 'em right, too."

"But we must make the best of both worlds, you know, Daniel," said John Trundle, finishing with a sort of little cough that meant—"It doesn't concern or scarcely interest me; only, others may be helped by the remark."

"Humph," said Dan'el, scratching his head for a few seconds, and turning it over. "That isn't Scripture, John."

John started. He had a faint idea that it was

somewhere in the Book of Proverbs. "No, John, no.
I don't know it; an' I don't believe it either. But
there—if it was, I fancy it would be well thumbed,
an' these kind o' worldly religious folks would call
that their favourite passage. An' what would they
mean by it? Why, that you're bound for to get so
much o' this here world as ever you can; an' just
so much o' the next world as is wanted for to make
it all right if death was to take 'ee unawares. No.
There isn't *two* worlds—only *one*. An' the only
world that you and I have got to live in is where we
can do the will o' the Father as it is done in heaven."

"Well, but it says *be diligent in business*," said
John, nodding his head with a sort of triumphant
certainty this time.

"It do, John, an' it do mean it too—*not slothful
in business.* Folks who don't put their heart into
their work, don't serve the Lord. Idlers an' drones
and them that can't buckle to and do a downright
good day's work, is poor Christians—hardly worth
the name."

"But the difficulty that I find is this," said young
Captain Joe: "diligence in business is apt to take
such a hold o' your thoughts that somehow or other
it pushes everything else out o' mind; and you are
carried away until there is scarcely any thought or
any heart left for anything else. I've found it so,
I'm sorry to say."

"Iss—and so have I, Cap'n Joe. But 'tis only because we put asunder what God have joined together. Seemin' to me, friends, that this here 'Not-slothful-in-business' is like Adam in the garden of Eden. He's put there for 'to dress it and to keep it.' But God says: 'It is not good that the man should be alone; I will make him an help meet for him.' And so the lovin' Father sends the fair *Fervent-in-spirit* to be joined in matrimony 'long with this *Not-slothful-in-business*. Then when they do take each other, an' do love an' honour an' cherish each other, they'll go on well, 'serving the Lord.' *Not-slothful-in-business* is a poor bachelor. He is like some sheep that are very good kind o' sheep, only they will break the fence, and so they must be coupled. Couple en up with *Fervent-in-spirit* an' they'll go well together."

Then Dan'el turned again to the Bible. "But, friends, I wanted to say a word or two more about this story o' Lot. Sodom must have had a bad name even then. And Lot had religion enough to make him feel a bit uncomfortable, I expect, before he could go right down amongst 'em and live there. I do believe, friends, that we lose ever so much o' the meaning o' the Bible because we go forgettin' that folks in them there old times was made o' just the same flesh an' blood, as we are now-a-days. An' Lot talked the matter over with his wife just the same as them that are like him do talk to-day: I can a'most hear 'em: 'Well,' says Lot, 'I can't help thinkin', dear, that 'tis really quite providential that this matter should have happened right here in sight 'o this beautiful place.' For Providence with these folks is *what pays*. I knew one of 'em once; he bought a share in a mine down here. Well, so long as ever the mine was a-paying dividends, 'twas such a merciful providence that he was led to buy that share. But when tin went down, an' there was no dividend,—then he feared that he had gone out of his providential path! Their providence haven't got anything to do with tribulations and trials."

Widow Pascoe sighed and shook her head.

"And so it haven't got anything to do with triumphs an' glorious victories either. No, 'tis nothing but makin' money an' gettin' on.

"And if Lot's wife were like the women be now-a-days—some of 'em, I mean—I do know what she would say. She'd say, 'Yes, dear—it does seem so. An' it will be such a pleasant place for the girls, too. Their Uncle Abraham is very good, and all that, you know; but it really is very dull for 'em, poor dears, dreadfully dull. They'll get to know some nice pleasant families, I hope, an' mix a little in society. O' course we must be careful! the place has not got a very good name.'

" ' Iss, we must,' says Lot, feelin' uncomfortable;
' it have got a very bad name indeed.'

" ' But it is *so* well watered,' says his wife.
' And we must not be uncharitable enough to believe
all that people say, you know. Besides, think o'
what a sphere of usefulness we shall have down
there ! '

" Ah ! Lot, you shall only escape by the skin o'
your teeth. But as for your wife, she shall perish
there—turned into a pillar of salt ; neither in Sodom
nor out of it, but between the two, like a monument
put up for to show what do come o' tryin' to make
the best o' both worlds."

Widow Pascoe sighed again deeply. The women
always did get the worst of it according to Dan'el.

Then Dan'el closed the Bible and spoke very
gravely :

" There ; I've tried to say what was 'pon my
mind. Now the Lord send it home to our hearts.
Seemin' to me, that 'tis wanted a'most everywhere,
and up here to Penwinnin just so much as anywhere
else. Let us take it to ourselves. This Lot was
religious, a just man an' a godly man ; but for all
that, you see, he was too much o' a worldly man, an'
it was nearly the death of him. I believe 't would
have been, but for Abraham. On here in the nineteenth chapter it do say that when God destroyed
the cities o' the plain, He *remembered Abraham*

8

and sent Lot out o' the place. The fact is, that 'tisn't enough for a man to get a bit o' the fear o' God in his heart, or a bit o' His love, an then to think that he can go on **lovin'** the world an' huggin' it up so much as he mind to. *Seek ye first the kingdom o' God* don't mean that we must first go and settle that matter once for all, and then 'tis all right for ever and we can please ourselves about how much o' the world we'll have. We must put it first, *an' keep it there;* or depend 'pon it that we shan't keep it at all. *Seek ye first the kingdom of God, and His righteousness; and all these things shall be added unto you.*"

John Trundle nodded his head and repeated the words, as his hand played with his gold chain, "*all these things.*"

"'All these things,'" Dan'el went on as if he had not **heard John's voice**—"but see what the promise is." And the Bible was opened at the sixth chapter of St. Matthew's Gospel. "Not ever so much money an' land an' a fine house an' costly clothes an' dainty meats an' drinks. No, no. The Heavenly Father do love His children too much for to promise us things like that. Enough **to eat**, enough to drink, and **enough to put on**: that's the '*all these things.*' An' I'm certain that there never was a man yet that put the kingdom o' God an' His righteousness in their proper place, but he had them three. An' there never was a wise man yet that havin' them three went frettin' for more.

" But 'tis that *first* that I do want us to mind. ' Seek ye *first* the kingdom of God, and His right-eousness.' While I been readin' the story o' Lot an' Abraham I've thought 'pon it again an' again. Here's a man that put the gain first, an' he lost all that he had twice over. Here is a man who wanted nothin' but an altar for the Lord an' a tent for his own self, and God made him one o' the greatest men that ever lived—the father o' kings and o' peoples. Do mind it, friends. Put the kingdom o' God an' His righteousness *first*. Not the well-watered field, nor the good wages, nor anybody's favour—but *first* the kingdom o' God. If 'tisn't there it will soon be nowhere.

" I don't know much about the ways o' queens an' knights an' such like. But I was thinkin' of it like this : Here comes Her Majesty 'pon the horse, and here's the knight : he've got the bridle, an' he's walkin' along by her side, carryin' his jewelled cap in his hand ; an' he's all eyes for his gracious Queen, an' is so quick an' graceful. There, that's a pretty pictur' of a good knight.

" But what do 'ee think o' this ? Here's the knight up on the horse his own self. ' Where's the Queen, Sir Knight ? ' ' O, she's comin' on behind somewhere ! '

"An' there she is, pickin' her way through the mud an' pushin' her way through the crowd ! Why, friends, I never did try my hand at that sort o' thing, but I think I'd have that traitor off that horse in a minute, an' I'd go down an' be the Queen's knight myself, clumsy old fellow as I am, afore I'd see her treated like that. Well, so long as our Religion is up on the horse an' we're waitin' 'pon her, we shall go the way Abraham went. But when this here self of ours is stuck up ridin' about, carin' for nothin' but gain or comfort or pleasure, an' only lookin' back over the shoulder to see if our Religion is comin' on behind all right through the mud an' the crowd—don't wonder if she's gone. She won't put up with that. And don't wonder either if thou art clapt into the dungeon 'pon bread an' water as thou dost deserve. 'Tisn't enough to be religious. We must put religion *first*, an' keep it there ; or depend 'pon it, friends, we shan't keep it at all."

VI

Dan'el's Notions about Preaching.

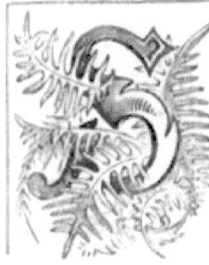UNDAY at Penwinnin was a fair specimen of "the Lord's Day" in the mining districts of Cornwall. A sacred stillness rested upon everything, strangely impressive after

hearing through day and night the roar of the stamps, and the clank and clatter of the other mine machinery. In place of the miners in red-stained dress, with the candle stuck in front of the hard round hat, with pick and borer and powder-tin on the shoulder, there came to-day groups of serious looking men, in sober black. The merry mine-maidens who had gone to and fro with their large, loose sun bonnets, appeared now in colours bright and gay as their own ruddy cheeks, and with ribbons too profuse and brilliant, perhaps, to please a severe taste.

The stillness seemed to give a new charm to those grand old granite hills, standing out in the calm, clear air, so sharply cut and so richly coloured, against a sky of the deepest blue. Is it the nearness of the sea, or is it the frequent rain that gives such a depth of colour, such greens to the grassy slopes, such a vivid yellow to the furze, such colour even to the rocks, hoary with lichens of daintiest hues, the patches of deep orange relieved by velvet borders of dark moss?

But already the earliest comers gather about the door of the little whitewashed chapel—the women going in and taking their places on the free seats on "the women's side;" the men standing about the door, as if somewhat shy of entering by themselves.

Rapidly the worshippers arrive now, for Dan'el

is to preach this morning, and he is a great favourite : the place **will** be filled, aisles and all. Curious
hearers of the well-to-do class come up from Redburn. Homelier groups come down from the little
cottages perched in queer, out-of-the-way places, by
narrow roads between the thick, high hedges that
shut them in—hedges whose banks of moss are now
quite hidden by primroses and luxuriant clusters of
fern, whilst the sweet breath of violets scents all the
air. Others come through the fields, over the awkward stiles and past the refuse heaps of old mine
workings and perilous shafts, half-hidden by thick
growth of bramble.

As **we go** on together, good reader, it **will be**
worth while to hear Dan'el's notions about **preach-**
ing; notions that had often been turned **over, well**
hammered out and very firmly held. It was as he
cobbled away one Monday morning that a talk of
the previous day's sermon with young Cap'n Joe,
gave an opportunity of expressing his opinions on
this matter.

" Well, Cap'n Joe, my advice to everybody is
this: *Don't* **you** *preach* **if** *you can help it.* 'Tisn't
enough for a man to want to preach. Nor yet for
a man to fancy that he could preach. If that was
all, good Preachers would be so common as black-
berries. An' 'tisn't enough for other folks to think
that a **man's got a** call to preach either; though

there is something in that. No; afore ever a man have got any business in the pulpit, he must feel like it was 'long with Jeremiah the prophet. You know, he thought he'd give up preachin', an' take his name off the plan. *I will not make mention of Him, nor speak any more in His name:* that is what he said. An' if a man *can* hold his tongue an' be comfortable about it, 'tis the best thing he can do: there's gabble an' cackle enough in the world a'ready, what with geese and other folks. But, bless 'ee! Jeremiah could no more hold his tongue than he could fly: *His word was in mine heart as a burning fire shut up in my bones, and I was weary with forbearing, and I could not stay.* There: when a man do feel like that, he'll preach somehow: he *must.* An' if a man have never felt like that, well, the Heavenly Father may have meant him for a decent shoemaker, Cap'n Joe, or a carpenter or somethin' o' that sort; but he was never meant for a Preacher 't all, an' nobody could ever make a Preacher out of him either.

"Why, you can tell 'em in a minute—a'most before they do open their mouths; for there's nothing in this world that's further off from each other than them two: the Preacher that men do make and the Preacher that is sent by God. I've noticed that the old prophets always had ' *a burden* ' afore they spoke. Like as if the message o' the Lord laid

heavy upon 'em, an' pressed them day an' night.
That's the difference, Cap'n Joe, between men that
can preach an' men that can't. The prophet that
is come from the Lord do feel the truth all over
him. It do take up all his thoughts, an' do press
'pon his heart, givin' him a thrill o' joy in it his own
self, or else makin' him tremble at it with very fear.
It'll be ringin' in his ears day an' night, a-followin'
him wherever he goes, an' whatever he's a-doin' of.
Why, when the Word o' the Lord comes 'pon me
like that, I can't help hammerin' my shoes to the
text that I got runnin' in my mind, an' stitchin'
'em with it, like as if it was the application. The
very clock will keep tickin' it in my ears, an' a'most
everything that I see do come to be mixed up with
it. There 'tis, seemin' to me: the Word must be
a burnin' fire shut up in the man's bones; an' then
he'll preach, then he'll preach." And Dan'el tapped
away at the sole as if that settled the matter.
Cap'n Joe was turning the notion quietly over in
his mind, without saying a word. Presently Dan'el
looked up again, the little eye twinkling merrily:

"An' talking o' bones do put me in mind of
another thing. I've heard tell about *Skeleton Sermons*. Now, seemin' to me, Cap'n Joe, that there's
only one way for a sermon not to be a skeleton. It
must come out of a man's own heart, wrapt up in
his own flesh an' blood, an' breathin' with the man's

own life. If it don't, then there'll be bones; dead bones; nothing but bones. Put together all in order, I dare say, but bones only, Cap'n Joe, for all that. No naturalness about 'em—I do mean no life an' no realness, but a sort of a ghostly thing that you can see through. All varnished an' shinin', may be, but dead bones still. Why, I should every bit so soon expect for to see a passle o' skeletons a-walkin' about, as to meet them there kind o' good people that you hear about sometimes from the pulpit, or them there dreadful sinners. I should so soon expect for to see a skeleton standin' up to young Polsue's smithy a-pullin' the bellows, or to see a couple of 'em sittin' down here alongside o' me, mendin' shoes, as to see them there kind o' sermons anywhere out o' the pulpit. They'm skeletons, Cap'n Joe; an' all they're good for is to be kept locked up in a box, and brought out every two or three years, so dead as dust an' so proper as nothin'. There's no life in 'em; no kind o' brotherliness for to shake hands with 'e an' for to wish anybody brave speed. I've very often thought when I've been listenin' to 'em that these here kind o' skeleton sermons would do very well perhaps for a lot o' skeletons to listen to if you could only get 'em together: very good for them that aren't troubled with any flesh an' blood, an' so haven't got to work for their bread an' cheese, an' never need a new suit o' clothes, much less a button put on or a pair o' stockin's for to be mended. You see, Cap'n Joe, **if you** happen for to step 'pon their corns, why, they can't feel it, an' that makes a deal o' difference; **so** 'tis **no** wonder that they do stand all the day long smilin' with such a lovely smile, like as if nothing couldn't put 'em out.

"Though, there—it won't do for me **to set** myself up for knowing how to do it better than other folks; but I have **learnt this** here lesson: A man may think about his text so much as ever he mind to, an' **get** ever so much light 'pon it; but when he've made his cake, he must take an' bake it down by the fire o' his own heart: and that do mean that he've got some fire down there. Skeletons haven't; **they'm all** head an' ribs. There 'tis, Cap'n Joe, depend 'pon it. A man must take the text down to his own heart an' find out what 'tis to his own self: then he can talk about it. He must get the Blessed Lord to be to his own soul what he is tellin' about to other people; then it'll come for to have some real flesh an' blood an' life about en. Never mind what a man do think or **what** he do see; my belief is that he can't *preach* any more o' the Gospel than he have got in his own heart."

Dan'el set down the worn out boot that he was patching, and took up the Bible that always lay near at hand.

"Here, Cap'n Joe, if you do want to find how

the Lord do make Preachers, an' where they are to get their sermons from, 'tis in the fifth o' Mark, an' somewhere about the nineteenth verse."

" About the man that had the devils cast out of him," said Cap'n Joe, as he found the place.

" Iss, that's it.   You see, he wanted to be with Jesus, but I expect he was too old for to go to College, an' Jesus said to him : ' Go an' tell the people what great things the Lord hath done for thee, and hath had compassion upon thee.' That's the only kind o' Preacher : he that can tell about the Lord Jesus because He has done great things for the man his own self. He can tell how kind an' lovin' an' gentle Jesus is, because He had compassion upon him. Then it will come up like the water in a spring, fresh and clear an' delicious. An' like I've heard tell o' water too, it do always find its level. If a sermon do come from the lips an' no deeper, it'll get to the ear an' no further. An' if it do come from the head, it'll get into the head an' soon be out again most likely. But if it do come from the heart, Cap'n Joe, depend 'pon it it will get to the heart and be there a well o' water springing up into life. Iss, that's it, I'm sure, Cap'n : as a man ' thinketh in his heart, so is he ' : and according to what a man's got in his heart so will he preach. If there's nothing in there but old blessin's that come years ago, then there'll be nothing but old sermons. That's how 'tis that there do come to be dry Preachers: they haven't been drawin' any water lately for their own selves out o' the wells o' salvation. 'Tis a pity that the Lord's ambassadors should ever come to be like them wily fellows o' Gibeon, that took old sacks 'pon their asses, an' wine bottles, old au' rent, an' old shoes an' clouted 'pon their feet, an' all the bread 'o their provision was dry and mouldy. However good it was once, though it was took hot out o' the oven, the bread will get dry an' mouldy if you do keep it long enough: an' so will sermons too. A Preacher is a man who do want anointin' with fresh oil once a week to keep en from dryin' up. Seemin' to me that it ought to be now like it was 'long with the people o' Israel: they was fed with manna that come down from Heaven fresh an' new every mornin'. David wanted new joys before he could preach, an' so do we too."

And Dan'el hammered away again, nodding his head as if that matter was settled beyond all doubt, and he wasn't going to hear a word more about it.

"You're right, Dan'el. I can see it plain enough," said young Cap'n Joe. "'Tis true, every word of it."

"Iss, an' there's another thing about gettin' the truth into other people's hearts. I've heard folks talk about *preachin' at people*, like as if it was the dreadfulest thing in all the world. Why, 'tis the only kind o' preachin' that is worth the name. Pick 'em out an' aim *at* 'em so straight as ever you can. What! go shootin' an' not shoot *at* the bird. Fire under en or above en or all round en; anywhere except *at* en, for fear o' hittin' en an' bringin' en down! That's playin' the fool when 'tis for sparrows · an' blackbirds; but when you are only trying to bring down men an' women 'tis quite fitty au proper! Pack o' stuff an' nonsense! Why, I can't preach a morsel if I don't preach straight at people. When I'm a-turnin' over the text I do try an' pick out what'll suit us over here to Penwinnin, an' preach accordin'. I do go over the congregation, an' ask the Blessed Lord to give me a word for them, one by one; you among the rest. An' I do think what there is in it for one an' another; what comfort there is in it for old Widow Polsue; an' what bit o' help for one or two that have had plenty to make 'em feel a bit down. There's one seekin' the Lord, an' he do want a bit of encouragin'; an' there's another do want a word o' warnin', for the world is swallowin' en all up. And then I got to look about an' find a morsel for the children. An' poor Bob Byles' wife tryin' to keep up as she is with all her little ones. I must get a word o' comfort out o' it for her. An' you must hold it out straight to 'em, Cap'n Joe, if you do mean 'em to take it. If you don't, they are sure to think that 'tis for somebody

else. Iss, good powder **an' shot** is often lost for
want of a good aim—an' so is a good many sermons.
Preach at the folks, Cap'n Joe—straight at 'em.

"**An'** mind not to forget the windows. Be sure
o' that. Every sermon ought to be builded like the
Lord told Noah to build the ark—*a window shalt
thou make in the ark.*"

"Windows, Dan'el!" said Cap'n Joe, looking
up perplexed. "**What** are they?"

Dan'el turned from his work and pointed to the
little window, crowded as it was with tools and
scraps of leather and odds and ends. "Why, for to
let the light in through, to be sure, Cap'n. An' not
only for to let light in—a skylight **would** do that
well enough. See how nice it is to *look out through,*
an' to see my little bit o' garden, an' Farmer **Gribble's** fields, with the daisies an' the buttercups, an'
the lambs a-friskin' about. That's what windows
are for, in houses an' sermons too, Cap'n Joe."

"You mean illustrations, Dan'el?"

"**O' course** I do! An' a sermon without them **is**
like **a house without windows.** Everybody must ha'
noticed how the Blessed Jesus kept tellin' the people
about the lost sheep, **or the** prodigal son, or the
faithless steward, or the ten virgins. An' how He
kept saying, "The kingdom o' heaven is like" this
an' like that. Folks will always prick up their ears
so soon as ever the Preacher do begin with his *likes.*

Why, I can't help thinkin' that half the purpose o'
the grand old stories in the Bible, about Goliath, and
Samson, an' Joseph, an' David, about Moses and
Elijah an' Dan'el is for that very thing : for to make
windows with 'em.   Poor old Clyma, down to Redburn, built a house an' forgot any window in one o'
the rooms, an' he never heard the last of it."

"Yes, I've often heard of that as a joke against
old Simon," said Cap'n Joe.

"Well, for my part, I do believe a man do make
every bit so big a blunder for to build a sermon
without any illustrations. Why, nine folks out 'o
ten aren't accustomed for to think over things at
all ; an' the machinery that they've got for to think
with is all rusty for want o' use.   'Tis no good
sayin' that they ought to be made to think : you
must make the best o' what you got.   An' there's
women and children, why, if the Preacher do go
argeyin' it out, they're sure to get nothin' out o'
that.   But they are used to *seein'* things : every one
o' them can look 'pon a picture.   Put in a story, or
one o' the Blessed Master's *likes*, and it'll be a window for to let the light in through ; an' if you mind
to make it so, 'twill be a window for to let 'em look
out through too 'pon a pretty little bit of a view.   I
do know that there's high an' mighty folks that
pretend for to think that preachin' like that isn't
learned, an' all that.   They do like something that

nobody can't understand. But I'm sure that 'tis a brave deal better for to try an' be like the Blessed Master. Seemin' to me as if He Who taught us how to pray have *showed* us how to preach. An' depend 'pon it we can't do better than sit down at His feet in this as in everything else, an' learn of Him Who is ' meek and lowly in heart.' "

Then Dan'el turned to his work. " But there, Cap'n Joe, this here is only my opinion after all. Let other folks have their notions and stick to 'em. There's heaps o' people that I can't do no good to, an' so I s'pose that we do want different sorts o' Preachers for different kind o' hearers. There is some that can't eat nothing but gingerbread trade 'long with gilt stuck all over it. An' there's some that will spend all their money 'pon nuts that there's no crackin'. An' there's other folks again that would sooner have a hot pasty with good beef an' 'taties in en ; an' I'm one o' them there."

" Well, Dan'el, there's no accounting for tastes," said young Cap'n Joe, laughing.

" No; 'specially when people haven't got no appetite an' no relish either, Cap'n Joe," Dan'el added, joining in the laugh. For a minute or two he bent over his work again ; then looking up, he finished the talk in a tone much more serious than that in which he had spoken before.

" But there—I'm sure that I'm not clever enough

nor anyhow fit for to give my advice. I could never
preach my own self like I wanted to, much less like
I ought to; an' what I've done in that way is fine
an' wished, sure 'nough, full o' faults an' failin's.
But I *have* tried for to make the Word plain and
simple, so that folks could understand it. 'Tis a
terrible thing, Cap'n Joe, an' it do often make me
tremble when I do hear Preachers preachin' in this
here grand an' highflown style. When the Lord
have set a watchman for to give warnin', if his
Master have given 'en a silver trumpet, by all means
let en use it—maybe some folks that are very particular about the looks and sound o' things will take
more notice of it than they would of an old ram's
horn like mine is. But whether 'tis 'pon ram's
horns or 'pon silver trumpets, do let a man take care
that he sounds it out plain, so that folks can be sure
o' what he means. I've heard folks, an' generally
with nothin' but ram's horns either, try to sound the
warnin' with so many twists and twirls an' shakes
an' flourishes, an' grand kind o' runnin' up an' down,
that you couldn't make anything out of it; only
like as if he was tryin' for to make folks think how
lovely he was playin', an' thinkin' about the collection afterward. When I do hear them kind o'
Preachers, I do feel a'most ready for to think o'
what the Bible do say o' Judas : *His bishoprick let
another take.*"

VII.

We Worship at Penwinnin, and hear Dan'el Preach.

T is time for us to enter the chapel, if we hope to secure a seat, for the little place is already nearly filled.

Looking around at the uneven white-washed walls, one's first thought is that whatever else may have attracted the people it certainly cannot be the beauty of the building. A plainer place could scarcely be imagined. At one end of it is the pulpit—an absurdly high box that reaches almost to the ceiling; the Bible, well worn and with many loose leaves projecting beyond the gilt edges, resting with the Hymn-Book on a cushion of faded velvet. Round the chapel there is a row of hat pegs now more than filled—piled up with hats and caps and a motley collection of head-gear. The pews are tall and high, ugly and uncomfortable, as if designed to render sleep impossible for the drowsy hearer. They stand with a stiff and Pharisaic contempt for the bare and backless forms in front and on either side of them, which are set apart as the free seats. A little gallery opposite the pulpit completes the heavy and ungainly appearance of the place.

But, good reader, do not despise these little whitewashed chapels which dot the bleak hill-sides of Cornwall, or cluster in the villages. Ugly and old-fashioned though they be, yet they are hallowed places, and many in heaven look down and hold them dear and sacred, second only to that Celestial City itself, paved with gold, and with gates of pearl. By all means let us have strength and beauty in the sanctuary—*strength* first and always; *then* beauty, too, if we can. He Who made the trees of Paradise not only " good for food," but also " pleasant to the sight," would have things fair and beautiful. Let us, however, be careful to imitate the wisdom and tenderness of our gracious Master: " I· have yet many things to say unto you, but ye cannot bear them now."

Do not let us carry our forms of worship any more than our religious teaching greatly in advance of the people, or we shall drive them from us. Better a hundred times that little place at Penwinnin, if people feel *at home* in it, than the most perfect Gothic structure, if they should sit uncomfortably subdued by a style of things to which they are all unused. Let rich Mr. Trundle and his fastidious daughters go to "church," as they threaten to do : that is a very little matter compared with the evil of having that plain, hearty, happy service at Penwinnin "churched" into stiffness and coldness and formality. It is very foolish to suppose that Gothic architecture, and stained glass windows, and syllabic tunes sung in "strict time," must of necessity do all this; but our wisdom lies assuredly, in not allowing either architect or choir-master to set the standard of taste ; nor the advanced worshipper, even though he be willing to pay for it. Let us study those for whom the place is built. They will go, and rightly too, where they can find homeliness and heart.

But Dan'el enters the pulpit, and the service begins. The opening hymn is a familiar one, and is sung to a familiar "trumpet metre" that always goes well. It told what Dan'el thought of the little chapel :

> " Lord of the worlds above !
>   How pleasant and how fair
> The dwellings of Thy love,
>   Thy earthly temples, are !

> To Thine abode My heart aspires
> With warm desires To see my God."

Everybody sings; heartily too, and in tune, the roll of the bass from "the men's side," and the clear treble of "the women's side," gaining each a richer fulness by the old-fashioned division. The tune is one in which the treble and bass part company for half a line, like a stream cleft by a rock, each holding on its way to meet again rapturously at the end of the verse. Well, it is bad taste to admire those old tunes with "their twists and their twirls an' their shakes an' their flourishes all up an' down," as Dan'el would say. Many of them certainly did run to absurd lengths; yet whether we have tunes ancient or modern, would that we always had such music in our worship and such heartiness as that with which the words ring out this morning !

> " The Lord His people loves ;
>   His hand no good withholds
> From those His heart approves,
>   From holy, humble souls :
> Thrice happy he, O Lord of hosts,
> Whose spirit trusts Alone in Thee."

And now Dan'el kneels in prayer. As he pleads, simply and earnestly with the Heavenly Father, an irregular volley of *Amen* rises from all parts of the chapel ; once or twice giving place to a rapturous *Praise the Lord !*

To you, good reader, this is perhaps more than unpleasant. You like something at least devout and orderly. This distracts your thoughts; it offends your sense of reverence. *The Lord is in His Holy Temple.* Well, they are an excitable and sometimes noisy people, these West Cornish Methodists; and there are times when the fervour and noise rise to a much higher pitch than on this Sunday morning. There is too, perhaps, a tendency to rest in such excitement; to let the religious life expend itself in such rapture. Yet it is only fair to ask ourselves, Where again can we find such a host of devout, praying, godly men as amongst these Cornish miners, born and bred amidst these noisy services?

And it may be well to ask further, whether intense religious feeling must, or can indeed, flow always in the channels that are dug for it? David danced with all his might before the Lord, much to the annoyance and vexation of his more æsthetic wife. And Abraham, that right reverend father, " fell upon his face, and laughed" when God gave him the promise of a son. And as to the Primitive Christians, there must have been no little noise in the streets of Jerusalem on the day of Pentecost when Peter had to make this defence of the disciples : " These are not drunken, as ye suppose."

At any rate, good reader, these Western folk have some real religion to make a noise over—and that certainly is better than that most dumb propriety without any religion, with which most of us are much more familiar.

Dan'el's text that morning was from Malachi iii. 10 : *Prove Me now herewith, saith the Lord of Hosts, if I will not open you the windows of heaven, and pour you out a blessing, that there shall not be room enough to receive it.*

Taking off the big spectacles, Dan'el laid them slowly beside him, and after a long pause burst out suddenly, in a tone that almost startled one, and in his sharp, jerky manner: " Friends, things 'long with Israel in Malachi's time was just the same as they be up to Penwinnin now—*wisht ; dreadful wisht.* An' for the same reason too. They forgot for to pay the Lord's dues."

Again Dan'el paused, and, in place of the sharpness, he spoke with tenderness and grief: " But there's one thing here that do come right to my heart. I can hardly think about anything else, friends. 'Tis this : *How the Lord longed for to bless them.* An', bless His name, He is just the same to us as He was to them. Ah ! friends, I believe 'tis a real grief to Him, and it do hurt His love when we shut the windows o' heaven. No wonder that we should pray to the Lord, poor an' needy as we are, an' dependin' 'pon His bounty for everything. But here is a wonder, sure 'nough—for here is the King

o' Glory a-beggin' an' prayin' of *us;* an' what for ?
Why, to let Him bless us like He wants to !

"Yet these were people that had done enough
to provoke Him past all patience. They had robbed
Him, an' He their lovin' and pitiful Father ! They
had gone tellin' lies about Him an' His blessed
service. They had cheated Him o' His tithes an'
dues. They had insulted Him with anything that
was poor an' bad an' torn an' worn out. And after
all that the Lord do speak all full o' pain an' grief.
He's longin' to have His son come back to His
heart again. *Return unto Me,* says He. And the
way He says it is all so grieved an' sorrowful that
it might break anybody's heart to hear Him ;—the
Lord open our ears to hear it. *Return unto Me, and*
I will return unto you, saith the Lord.

"And now, friends, I do want you to look well
at the text; long enough for to see this here very
plain. Folks can read a bill an' know all about it
to a ha'penny the first time o' goin' over it. I do
wish that they'd read their Bibles like they do their
bills. Then they would come to see something in
the text that most people don't think about. This
is what the Lord wanted the tithes for, because then
He *could open the windows o' heaven and send down*
a great blessin'.

"There's scores o' people do hear them words :
Bring all the tithes into the storehouse—an' then

they're off. They never think what 'tis for. Poor
things! the crack o' the Master's whip is in their
ears; an' they must dig an' sow an' reap an' bring in
the uttermost farthin'—like as if the Blessed Father
only wanted for to get out of us so much as ever He
could. If they waited long enough for to look at
the text they'd see very different from that. Bless
His name, what He wants is for to *give us so much as
we can carry away.* So He do ask for the tithes like
as if He wanted us to get rid o' some o' our common
stuff to make a bit o' room for His great blessin'.

" Why, down here, 'long with us, spite o' our
wants an' our greediness, 'tis more blessed for to
give than to receive. What must it be, then, with
the lovin' Lord Who gave *Himself* for us! how He
must long for to fill up all our wants! An' so He
do ask for the tithes, just like Elijah asked for the
first cake, but it was only that he might fill the
widow's barrel o' meal an' increase her oil. 'Tis
like the Blessed Jesus, sittin' there 'pon the well,
all thirsty an' tired. He says to the woman, ' Give
Me to drink.' But He was thinkin' about her all
the time, an' wantin' her to ask for a cup o' the
water o' life that she might never thirst any more.
Why, the Bible is full of it. 'Tis like the sons o'
Jacob when they went down to Egypt, and they took
a little present o' balm an' honey an' nuts, and they
brought it down to the palace o' this here great

prince. They were all so frightened, an' trembled
all over an' bowed their heads. But the prince
fetched 'em in to dinner with him, an' he filled their
sacks with corn. An' that wasn't half enough.
He fell 'pon their necks an' said, 'I am Joseph
your brother'; an' he couldn't rest till he had
brought them all down into the land o' Goshen to
live right there along with him. 'Tis just like that,
dear friends, with our lovin' Lord. 'Bring in the
tithes,' says He, 'that there may be meat in Mine
house,'—but He can't stop there, an' we mustn't
either,—' and prove Me now herewith, if I will not
open you the windows o' heaven, an' pour you out
a blessin', that there shall not be room enough to
receive it.'

"Now the Lord send the word home to our
hearts while we think o' these here three things.
First, *The windows o' heaven are shut over us.*
Second, *We have been and shut 'em our own selves.*
An' third, *The blessin' that'll come when once the
windows are opened again.*

" Well, friends, I'm 'fraid that there's no doubt
about the first thing—not a morsel. The windows
o' heaven be shut over us up here to Penwinnin.
The signs nowadays is just the same as they were
in the old time. There was the destroyer in the
fields. They might dig an' sow an' plant an' prune
so much as ever they mind to. But it all came to

nothin'. The frost killed half of it; and the worm was at the root, an' that killed a'most the other half. An' o' what managed to escape them, all the fruit fell off afore it was ripe. 'Tis 'zactly like that whenever the windows o' heaven are shut. We do preach an' pray an' work an' sow an' plant; but it do all come to nothin'. There's the frost in the air, friends: we'm all so cold an' stiff. There's a nippin', blightin' chill in folks. You can see it in their looks, and you can feel it in all their ways. They've a-got the east wind in 'em, and the good seed haven't got so much as a chance. And there's the worm at the root of it: ghastly old pride eatin' up everythin'—except the weeds; an' wretched old jealousy goin' about ill-wishin' it all. An' the east wind o' worldliness a-witherin' all the grace and spoilin' the King's garden.

"And what can we do for to keep these here dreadful things away? We can't turn the wind, an' fetch the breezes out o' the south. Patent ploughs an' clever farmin' won't keep off frost or stop the blight. The Lord must open the windows o' heaven. He must unlock His storehouse before ever we can get sunshine an' showers, an' good crops. An' that's true in the Church. We have got the old Gospel—thank God for it! But where's the old power gone to? We have got the same means o' grace; but they'm like Carwinnin stream in a hot summer—there's the old watercourse, but 'tis all dried up to nothin.' Iss, we got our Preachin' an' our Prayer-meetin' an' our Class-meetin' just the same, but they're so dead! Why, we can mind times up here—can't us, friends?— when the Word o' the Lord have burned like a fire ; when it have gone right through big sinners, like an arrow straight out o' God's bow, an' they've been struck down there an' then cryin' for mercy."

"Bless the Lord!" responded some old saint, fervently.

"Iss, times when nobody could get any rest, for them that had found the Lord was busy all day long a-teachin' them that was seekin' Him. Night an' day, home an' 'pon the road, sometimes in bed an' sometimes down the mine, the Spirit o' God was convincin' them o' sin, till a'most everybody you met could talk o' nothin' else but the way o' salvation."

Again came the response, but from half-a-dozen glowing hearts now.

"Why, I can mind when we've come together in this dear old place an' the glory o' the Lord have filled the house. Sing! you could hardly sing for tears o' joy an' gladness. Ah! some o' you can mind the times, friends—the King's banquetin' days—when it was like as if the Blessed Lord made a great feast, an' condescended so low as to ask us

poor folks up here to Penwinnin to come in 'long
with His lords and chief captains. An' He couldn't
do enough for us. 'Twas ask an' have what we
mind to, unto the half of His kingdom! Ah! an'
a long way more than that, bless Him! to sit in
heavenly places with Him, right up beside Him
'pon His throne!"

"Glory be to God!" rang from different parts
of the chapel, as many began to find something of
the old blessing in the memory of those better days.

"But there, 'tis wisht poor speed 'long with us
now, friends. An' this here is the reason of it : the
windows are shut—the windows o' heaven. People
do go puttin' it down to scores o' things that haven't
got no more to do with it than the man in the
moon. I'm a'most ashamed for to hear 'em go
talkin' about it as they do. 'Aw,' says one, 'the
times is altered. The old Gospel was all very well
for the old times, but we do want somethin' more.'
An' nowadays you mustn' expect to do no good
without you do go argeyin' agen all the other learned
folks an' provin' they're all wrong. Friends, don't
you believe such a pack o' nonsense. Our Master's
orders is just so plain now, an' just so bindin' too,
as when He was down here 'pon the earth : PREACH
THE GOSPEL. We got to stick to that. If that do
fail, well, that won't be our fault; but we haven't
got no business to go a-tryin' to tinker an' mend it

with our foolish ways an' doin's. Why, the very
bread a man eats might choke these lies in his
throat. Thousands o' years ago God made the
corn, and He put into it life enough for to last so
long as ever folks should want bread to eat. An'
let 'em get so rich or so learned or so anything else
as they mind to, bread they do want, an' bread is
life to 'em all the same. An' is the glorious Gospel
o' this same Blessed God so badly made that 'tis
worn out a'ready ? Is it so badly put together that
it'll break down an' all go to pieces so soon as ever
people do begin to think a bit. 'Tis nonsense. 'Tis
a'most blasphemy, for to go a-talkin' like that."

An' Dan'el stayed a moment as if he had to hold
back the indignation that stirred within him. He
tightened his lips and nodded his head as he went
on again :

" No, friends. There's only one reason. An'
the sooner we do see it, the sooner it'll be mended.
There ! " (and Dan'el pointed upward.) " There
—the windows o' heaven are shut. That's why
'tis. An' so there's no dew o' His blessin' 'pon the
Lord's field. There's no sunshine. There's no
showers for to water the earth. An' that's why 'tis
all so parched an' barren.

" Now the next thing about the windows o'
heaven is this here : *We have shut them over our
own selves.*

" 'Tis all our doin's, friends, an' nobody else's. We must see that plain, or we shall never mend matters 't all. An' 'tis a fine an' hard thing to see too; but 'tis true. I don't believe that the windows o' heaven have got any bolts or bars either 'pon the Lord's side. *We* shut them, an' *we* do put over the bolts. Why, there's such a weight o' blessin' heaped up 'pon them that the minute the bolts are pulled back, they are bound to fly open directly—they can't help theirselves about it.

" But if folks in those days were like they be hereabouts an' nowadays, I do know that they'd put the fault down to everything an' everybody sooner than to their own selves. I can hear 'em talkin' about it.

" ' Aw,' says one, ' windows o' heaven opened ! Why, 'tisn't a morsel o' good to expect that there ; not a morsel ; 'long with the preachers we got. If we only had a man like old So-and-so, or a Minister like Mr. Somebody, of Somewhere, there'd be a bit o' chance. But now !'—an' they'd fling up their head like as if you might so well expect the sky to fall as for the windows o' heaven to open. But see, friends, the Lord didn't send a Jonah to preach to them. The mischief wasn't to be mended that way 't all.

" ' Well,' says another, ' I dare say that there may be something in what Uncle John do say, but my 'pinion is this here : you can't expect for to get along, **an' to do** any great things, without you do get a new harmonium. Fiddles an' flutes is so old fashioned.'

"But see, friends, the Lord didn't **send another** David among 'em for to **drive the devil out with the** sound o' music.

"'Aw,' says another, ''tis **no** use talkin' like that. You do want a new chapel. 'Tisn't likely that you are a-goin' to have any great blessin' in a barn of a place—thatched and white-washed—like our chapel is.'

"Well, friends, **see again.** The Lord didn't say a word about that ; an' **I'm glad that He** didn't. Bless Him ! **Just as if He was not the same meek** and lowly Jesus **now** as when **He was** born in a stable an' laid in a manger.

"An' some o' the old folks would talk about it very serious, an' a'most make anybody think that the openin' o' the windows o' heaven depended 'pon the shape o' the bonnet or the cut o' the hair."

Widow Pascoe groaned a faint groan, and shook her head **very** solemnly.

"But the text have'nt got a word about that. This is all that the Lord told the people to do : to look after the duties that they'd forgotten. That was all : *to mend their evil manners;* then the windows would be opened right enough. He didn't

tell them to come up to chapel an' have a week o'
special services. 'Tis a capital thing, an' I'm not
goin' to say a word agen them; but there's one
thing better: 'tis better to go home an' serve the
Lord with all your heart all the week through. *Then*
come up with your special services to receive what
the Lord is sendin' down. 'Tis a good thing to
preach a rousin' sermon 'pon a Sunday evenin';
but mind, 'tis a good thing, too, for to go out 'pon
the Monday mornin' tryin' to please God an' to
glorify Him. 'Tis a good thing to pray in a Prayer-
meetin', *Lord, revive Thy work*: but if we do want
to have the windows o' heaven open, we must do
more than that, friends. We must keep our tempers.
We must pay our debts. We must be kind an'
patient au' lovin'. 'Tis the want o' *these* things that
do shut up the windows o' heaven. "Bring ye all
the tithes into the storehouse, . . . an' prove Me
now *herewith*, saith the Lord o' Hosts": *herewith*.

"But we must get up a bit closer to the windows,
friends, an' see what bolts these are, and who they
do belong to. Don't let us be too proud for to own
to it if they're yours an' mine. The Lord open our
eyes an' stir up our hearts."

Then Dan'el put on his spectacles solemnly and
looked up for a few seconds; his head turned a
little aside and his eye fixed as if trying to read
something.

" I'll read the names o' the bolts. Ah! there's one there; why, there's two o' the same sort—there's half-a-dozen o' them, an' more than that, an' they're all the same— *Hurried Prayer.*"

He took off his spectacles and looked around the chapel. " Now, who owns to that? Ah, friend, you can mind the time when it was well with the garden o' the Lord in your heart. 'Twas fenced off for the Blessed Master's own. Ah, an' what beautiful fruit there was : love, joy, peace! An' there was scarce an hour o' the day but you would hear His Blessed Voice as He walked in the garden. But now! now !—'tis all winter, isn't it? Trees stripped! flowers all dead an' gone! Now the place is all covered with dead leaves, and the winds do go a-howlin' an' moanin' about the place. Why, the very walls have tumbled down in a good many places, an' the world do come tramplin' all over the place like as if it hadn't got any Master for to take care of it. An' there's the reason of it all : you've got the great bolt up agen the windows o' heaven. You used to have a good time along with the Lord in the mornin'; now 'tis nothin' but a string o' words without a bit o' heart in 'em. Why, the Blessed Lord used to be so nigh at hand, an' the door was so easy for to open, that you could turn in a score o' times a day for a word with Him. But now—day after day, week after week, an' you don't hear His Voice or

find His Presence; like Absalom when he dwelt in
Jerusalem, but *saw not the face o' the king.* Come,
friend, thou must have at this bolt. Fetch en back.
Begin **again, in the old** ways, an' there'll be the old
blessin's **for thee. My Master** sends thee a challenge; wilt put Him to the proof? " Prove me
herewith," says He, "and see if I will not open *you*
the windows o' heaven.'

　　Again the spectacles were put on, and the face
was turned upward. He was silent for a few
seconds; then nodding his head three or four times,
he took off his spectacles and laid them by his side.
"Ah, friends, I thought it was that ! I've said to
myself half a dozen times lately, ' Depend 'pon it,
Dan'el, that somebody been puttin' that there bolt
agen the windows o' heaven.' And so they have;
there 'tis—*Want o' brotherly love.* With one 'tis
want o' patience; you've got all sharp-tempered
an' angry spoken, an' that's your bolt. Another is all
vexed with the neighbour next door, an' can't abide
for to think about en or to see en. With another
'tis a ghastly bit o' pride; an' they're too high an'
mighty for to notice anybody, much less for to shake
hands with 'em. Another have put up a bit o' unkind-
ness. You had a chance o' doin' somebody a good
turn, an' you wouldn't go half-a-dozen steps out o'
your way to do it—perhaps you went two or three
steps the other way to find an excuse for not doin' it.

"Now, perhaps you think that these are little matters that don't make any difference. Why, you know well enough that it don't take much for to bar the door with. And brotherly love is a thing that our Lord is so particular about that He won't let a man knock to the door o' heaven till he is in love an' charity with his neighbour; much less will He open the windows o' heaven for him. You may go on prayin' and thinkin' yourself wonderful religious, but 'tisn't a bit o' good so long as that bolt is up; not a bit. You go talkin' about your lovin' the Lord Jesus. Well, I shouldn't like for to say that you was a story-teller 'zactly; but this is what is wrote down in the Scripture: *If a man say, I love God, and hateth his brother, he is a liar: for he that loveth not his brother whom he hath seen, how can he love God Whom he hath not seen?*

"Friends, that bolt have got to come back. An' he may so well come first as last. 'Tis an awkward bolt to handle, too. But if you do only make up your mind about it, why, a word or a look will sometimes send en flyin' back in a minute. Come now, brother, wilt accept the Lord's challenge? 'Prove Me now *herewith*, and see if I will not open *you* the windows o' heaven.

"But, friends, there is just one more bolt I want for to say a word about! 'Tis the same as these people put up in the old times. An old rusty bolt

'tis. An' he's in so tight that there's hardly any
movin' of en. He must be oiled well before he'll
start. I'll read out the name of it, an' then you
that it do belong to can claim it for your own
selves."

Looking upward, with the spectacles drawn out
to the tip of his nose as if to see more distinctly,
Dan'el spelt out the name: " N-I-G—'tis a long
word, friends, an' I was never very much o' a hand at
long words : N-I-G-G-A-R-D-L-I-N-E-S-S. Ah !
that's it—*niggardliness*. Well, you'll have to grease
that bolt well with the oil o' liberality, an' have at en
with the sledge hammer o' the Word before ever
he'll start. But till he's back, friend, the windows
o' heaven will never be open. You do think o'
what you are savin'. Well, 'tis worth while to think
too o' what you are losin'. ' Prove Me now herewith,
and see if I will not open you the windows o' heaven,
an' *pour you out a blessing such that there shall not
be room enough to receive it.*' There! you're makin'
a bad bargain ; that is what you're losin', friend—
more than there's room to receive.

"But now I want to stir up our minds, dear
friends, by thinkin' o' what *the Lord will pour down
'pon us if only the windows be opened again.*
' Windows o' heaven '—well, here's a story for
you boys an' girls, so well as for us old folks.
Once 'pon a time there was a great city, an' a great

army came up against it for to take it. They couldn't
do that, so they said 'Let's starve 'em to death
then.' So they put a guard all round the place, an'
watched day an' night so that nobody shouldn't go
in or out, an' waited. Well, very soon all the food
in the city was eaten up, an' the people began to be
in dreadful want, sure 'nough, an' was mad with
hunger. The houses was all stript an' bare; an'
the faces was all pale an' hollow; the poor little
children was all cryin' an' dyin' o' very want.
Now when the king o' the city saw the dreadful
state o' things he got into a rage, an' said that
he'd kill the prophet o' the Lord for sendin' all
these troubles 'pon the people. An' away he
went with one o' his knights for to cut off the
prophet's head. But as he was comin' the prophet
saw him, an' cried out: 'By to-morrow this time
there shall be plenty o' bread, your majesty,—
enough an' to spare.'

"Why, where could it come from? All the
bread in the place was eaten up long ago; an' nobody could send them any help from outside. There
was only one way that it could come, an' the king's
servant turned up his lip an' sneered. 'Pooh,' says
he, 'if the Lord would make windows in heaven,
might this thing be.'

"Ah, friends, that's just what God was goin'
to do! Well, that night there was four poor lepers

sittin' in the gate o' the city, so miserable as ever
they could be. 'I wish I was dead,' says one.
'So do I,' says another. 'So I do too,' says both
the others. 'Well, things can't be no worse 'long
with us, come what will; so I'll tell 'ee what 'tis,
comrades. I'm goin' over to the camp o' the
enemy. If they do kill us, why, we shall only die
a bit sooner, an' if they save us alive, why there,
we shall live.' So away they go.

"'Tis just in the twilight. An' now they do
begin to get near to the camp an' feel a brave
bit frightened, I expect, for the sentinel will
be walkin' up an' down, an' he may send a spear
a-whizzin' right through 'em afore they know it.
But as they do come creepin' along, one tumbles over
something lyin' 'pon the ground. He picks it up
an' 't is a lovely robe. Another kicks somethin' that
goes ringin' an' shinin'. 'Tis a lovely gold cup.
Then another do find somethin' better still; an' that's
a loaf o' bread. But there was not a man in the
place; only horses tied an' asses tied an' tents all
standin', an' all sorts o' things lyin' about 'pon the
ground. So there they was with plenty o' bread
an' meat an' a good appetite, too, an' nothing to
pay; so if they didn't make a good meal 't was
their own fault.

"'But, stop,' says one o' them, 'there's our
poor starvin' neighbours home. Let us be gone

back an' tell them the good news. They'll hardly
believe their ears, will they?' So back they come,
an' knock to the gate o' the city. The old watchman wakes up all tremblin', an' thinkin 'tis the
dreadful soldiers come. 'Who's there?' he says,
tryin' to speak quite bold. Then in a minute he
hears the voice of these here lepers :

"'Open the gate, do'ee; for the enemy is clean
gone. An' they've left all their things behind 'em,
tents an' clothes an' bread an' meat an' all sorts.
An' there isn't a man left in the camp.'

"Well, the news spread like fire, an' out come
the folks an' found 'twas all true. The enemy *was*
gone. So every one o' them helped hisself to
what he mind to; an' by daylight there was flour
so cheap as ever. Ah! the Lord had made windows in heaven, an' there come a dreadful noise that
frightened the enemy all out o' their wits. Every
man o' them took to his heels so fast as ever he
could run, an' never dared so much as to look behind
en. Flingin' away cloak and cup, sword an' spear,
away they went, helter-skelter for their very lives.
There, *that's* havin' the windows o' heaven opened ;
an' that's what the Blessed Lord is waitin' an'
wantin' to do for us. No more folks goin' about
among us, groanin' 'My leanness, my leanness,'
but bread enough an' to spare. No more folks
grumblin' agen each other because things is come

to such a pitch; but every man happy an' blessin' the Lord. No more the old enemy gettin' the upper hand o' us an' threatenin' every day for to be the death o' us; but, instead o' that, the enemy bruised under our feet. Bless the Lord, 'tis comin', 'tis comin'! My Lord, we will take up the challenge, an' put Thee to the proof. An' before the day is over Thou wilt send the glory. Back with the bolts, comrades; every man back with his bolt. Down 'pon our knees before the Lord, an' get the windows opened; an' before the week is over the power will come. The Lord send the Word home. Amen!"

And Dan'el closed the book amidst the fervent response of "Amen!" as it rose from almost every heart in the place.

Dan'el has a Visitor.

THE morning after the sermon Dan'el was seated at his work humming to himself a favourite old tune. Suddenly the upper half of the door leading into the shoemaker's shop was opened, and Farmer Gribble appeared in the doorway.

A man by himself in the village was Jeremiah Gribble; as distinct from the people of Penwinnin as if he had come from the other side of the earth. Yet his birthplace was only some forty miles away in the eastern part of the county—an unknown region which the neighbours spoke of rather contemptuously as "up the country," or occasionally

as " up in England "; whilst with the old folks
Farmer Gribble was described as coming from
" them foreign pairts," which was exactly synonymous
with the phrase " haythen lands."

For five and forty years " ould Mest' Gribble,"
as he was called, had lived amongst these people,
yet his brogue, his dress, his very " looks," were as
distinct from those about him as on the day of his
coming amongst them. Short, stout, red-faced—
you saw at a glance that he did not belong to the
same race as these miners : tall and slender, square-
shouldered and pale-faced as they were. Then he
was almost alone in the parish as a real farmer,
where others added the care of a couple of fields and
a cow or two to the work of mining. A strict
Churchman in a land of Methodists, he was, except
the clerk, the only regular attendant at the parish
church, for the sexton himself went off to the chapel
as soon as he had finished tolling the bell.

Then, again, his East-Cornish dialect was
almost as perplexing to these West-countrymen as
a bit of Yorkshire ; and there was a mutual and
undisguised ridicule at what each spoke of as the
" redicklus pernounshiation " of the other.

But it was in the strictness of his Church notions that Farmer Gribble differed most widely from
his neighbours. To his mind the parish Clergyman
was the embodiment of all authority, and religion in

the main was to abide by what he said and did. In
addition to this there was thrown in as a make-
weight the due attendance at "Prayers" on Sunday,
and the penance of listening to a twenty minutes'
sermon. Whatever religious observances ventured
beyond this limit were not only needless, but
amounted to a heresy of which the farmer drawled out
an angry condemnation. His red face grew redder,
and his short hair seemed to bristle all over his cheeks
and on his round head as he protested against it :

"Voaks ought tew mind what Paul zaith—zaith
he, 'Yew muzzen be righchus ovver much.'" (All
Scripture with Farmer Gribble was conveniently in-
dicated by reference to Paul.) "Theare es waun
gude theng onder the zon, and thickey's a bit ov
religion—I dew mane *Church,* ov course. And then
there es tew bad thengs—haven' noan and a-haven'
tew much. Anoff es so gude as a vaiste, and tew
much es a'moast so bad as noan."

The good Clergyman preached on the Sunday
morning in an adjoining parish, and then gave the
afternoon to the half-dozen souls that made up the
congregation at Penwinnin, where he lived. But it
would not be right to let the reader imagine for a
moment that the dear old Vicar was to blame for
such a flourishing of dissent. The state of things
had come about before his time; and after three
generations of these people had grown up in the life

and glow of their hearty services, it was no easy matter to win them back to the beautiful but more cold and stately form of the Church service. A man of blameless life, he moved in and out amongst them beloved and honoured, welcomed always in his visits at their houses; and whilst there were many things that were not to his taste, yet a Christian first and then a Churchman, he rejoiced that Christ was preached, and that the Gospel was "the power of God unto salvation" to hundreds about him.

For Farmer Gribble to go out of the parish even to hear his own Minister was a bit of zeal that would smack of that overmuch religion which he denounced as heresy. So it came about that, for want of something better to do, he sometimes dropped in at the little chapel on the Sunday morning, carefully abstaining, however, from sharing a hymn-book, as a protest against being regarded as a regular member of the congregation. He had been one of Dan'el's hearers on the previous morning.

This morning the farmer had brought with him a leather strap that needed a few stitches from the shoemaker.

"Good mornin'," said Dan'el, looking up from his work for a moment. "Good mornin', Mest' Gribble; come in, Sir."

For a minute the farmer stood at the opened

doorway, quite still and without a word. Dan'el
had turned to his work again before the answer
came. First there was a deep sigh; then he spoke
with a slower, heavier drawl than usual, scratching
his head as if to stir up his wits. "I 'moast a-
vorgot what I comed for. Tez the strap; et wan'th
a stitch or tew, zo Bill zaith."

Then the farmer came slowly inside the door,
and handing the strap to Dan'el, he sat down on a
little stool opposite to the shoemaker.

"That's soon done," said Dan'el, picking up the
tools for the work. A few holes thrust through
with his shining awl, a vigorous tugging of the stout
thread, and it was finished.

"There, Mest' Gribble; if broken hearts were
mended so easy as that, 'twould be a different world
from what 'tis."

The farmer had risen to leave, but he suddenly
sat down again, as if Dan'el's words had not only
struck, but hurt him too.

Dan'el lifted his face, wondering what ailed the
farmer. Then as if he had no more time to think
about it, he bent over his work again with new
vigour. It was after a longer silence that the farmer
spoke this time, and in a tone that made Dan'el look
up with a new interest in his visitor.

"Dan'el, yew nevir zaid a truer word."

Dan'el had almost forgotten what he had said.

Fixing his eye upon the farmer as if reading his soul, he asked with surprise, " Why, Mest' Gribble, what do you know then about broken hearts? I thought you didn't hold with them 't all."

Farmer Gribble's eyes were fixed on the floor, and he was vigorously pushing his foot with the end of his walking-stick. His old roughness of manner returned for a moment.

" No more I dew." But the sentence ended in another sigh, and after a long pause he went on again, in quite a different tone. " But yew dew, Dan'el—yew dew. An' yew'm so likely to be right as I be—every bit."

Dan'el stitched away quietly, as the most effectual way of drawing the farmer out; hopefully and thankfully guessing what it was that he had come to talk about. But the silence that followed was so long that Dan'el was just going to venture on another question, when his visitor sighed again, and worked away at the toes of his boot.

" Dan'el, tes uncommon hard for tew thenk anybody be wrang when he'th sticked to hes 'pinions for yeears, like a lempot."

" 'Tis, Mest' Gribble, sure 'nough," said Dan'el kindly. " I've found it so, fine an' often."

" Iss—tes, Dan'el, tes ; " and the farmer thrust and twisted his stick so violently that he might have been trying to make another job for repair. Then he put both hands on the top of the stick, and rested his chin on them. "Well—if yew'm right, then I dew reckon that I *be* wrang, Dan'el—*that* I dew:" and he nodded his head slowly by way of confirming it.

The old clock ticked solemnly in the corner, but there wasn't another sound, for Dan'el moved his hands noiselessly, eager to catch every word.

"I be a man that doan't hold weth tew much religion. No more I doan't hold weth goin' wethout any. But yesterday you made me veel I hadn't got noan my own zelf, an' never had noan neyther. And vexed enough I was with 'e; an' zo I be still."

Dan'el looked up with a smile, but the farmer's face was serious, and even sad.

"Never had noan," the farmer went on very slowly, shaking his head. "An' a-prided myzelf as I have a-done, tew!"

· Again he lifted himself, as if trying to throw off this weakness of his; but he leaned forward a moment after, and worked his stick into his foot once more. "It go'th agen the grain uncommon. But theare, if wrang I be, better tew zee it now than fur to zee it when et's tew late."

Dan'el did not look up from his work.

"Why, yew gived out the hymn like as if yew veeled it all over. An' yew prayed like as if yew'd com to know the Lord fur to speak tew. An'—an' —an' I *doan't*, Dan'el. I *doan't*."

x

Then the old man's voice grew husky, and tears came into his eyes, as he whispered, "And I dew wish I did, Dan'el—*that* I dew."

Dan'el bent over his work fairly bewildered. He had prayed earnestly about the service of the previous morning, and was looking for fruit from it; but somehow the thought of his old neighbour being laid hold of thus had not occurred to him. They had often talked together; but one might as well have tried to move a granite rock by argument as to move Farmer Gribble. And now that he was come in this way, whilst Dan'el rejoiced greatly in it as a token for good, yet he was at his wit's ends as to the best way of dealing with him. At last, half angry with himself, he laid down his work, and looked up quite ready to talk the matter over in good earnest.

"Well, Mest' Gribble, 't won't do for you to go by what I do say 't all. I'm so likely to be wrong as you, every bit. We must get right on to the Word to once."

—"An' regalar to the Church as I've a-been, tew!" said the old man, shaking his head. "To be wrang arter all! eh, dear! eh, dear!"

"Yes, it must be more than that—church or chapel either, or both together, for that matter," Dan'el replied.

But the Farmer went on as if talking to himself, paving no heed to Dan'el.

—" An' a-been so careful tew as I've a-been:
a-payin' everybody their due, an' all that! An' to be
wrang arter all—nort in it, nort!" And again his
his voice grew husky, and he shook his head and
sighed.

" Well, there is something in that, Mest' Gribble,
an' a good deal too; an' I wish folks would think
that there's more in it. A-payin' twenty shillin's
in the pound, an' a kind heart, an' a civil tongue in
your head, an' a clean pair o' hands that won't take
no more than their due, an' won't give no less—'t is
no good folks settin' theirselves up for religious if
they haven't got so far as that there. But all that
won't do instead o' love to God, Mest' Gribble.
That's the first an' great commandment: 'Thou
shalt *love* the Lord thy God with all thy heart.'
An' *love* is a kind o' thing inside o' a man, a-burnin'
an' a-glowin' all over en."

Farmer Gribble looked up, and reached out his
head intently. Crusty old bachelor as they reckoned
him, he too had gone through all the fiery discipline
of love; had flung up for it the estate that had been
in the family for generations; had left his father's
house and his kindred away up in that bleak parish
in the east of the county, and never set foot in it
since.

" Zay that theare agen, Dan'el, will 'e, plaise?"

" Nothin' can take the place o' love, Mest'

x 2

Gribble. God do *love* you an' me; an' love is a thing that can't rest nohow till it do get a bit o' real love back again. *Love must have love.* 'Tis like I've heard tell o' royalty, love won't wed with any but its own rank."

The old man nodded his head. "*Love must have love,*" he muttered to himself two or three times. Then he struck the floor with his stick. "Theare yew be right, Dan'el. Yew've a-hit the nail upon the head this time. To thenk that I never zeed it avore now! Arter all that I hev a-gone through, tew!" His voice sank to a whisper, and he shook his head sadly. "An' to thenk that the Lord in heaven hath been a-frettin' and a-grieven for my love. An'—an'—to thenk that I *doan't* love Him!" Again came a long pause and a deep sigh. "But I want tew, Dan'el; I *dew* want tew. Wull 'ee help me?" And the tears crept slowly down the old man's face.

Dan'el's heart was fairly roused to his work now. "Bless thee, dear old friend, I'll do something better than that! I'll go with thee to One Who can help thee indeed." And Dan'el quietly lifted up his heart for the light and guidance of Him Who is come to shed the love of God abroad in our hearts. As he spoke now the words came all aglow, and with a vigour and authority that Farmer Gribble at once yielded to and rested in with a childlike simplicity.

"Love must **have** love," the old man muttered to himself, nodding his head over the truth that had taken such **hold** of him.

"And there's another thing, Mest' Gribble, that's just so true as that there. I do often think about it, sittin' here to my work. Only love can 'make love,' as folks do say: anyhow **nothin'** but love can *wake* **up** love. You may shout to it, an' you may storm 'pon it, an' you may cudgel it, **but** that there 'll never wake love up—may kill poor **sleepin'** love, perhaps but won't do nothin' else. **You** may jingle gold in the ears o' it if you mind to, an' you may offer it ever so good wages—but, bless'ee, love 'll keep on sleepin' for all that."

Dan'el little thought how **readily the** farmer's heart opened to all his words, and **how much there** was there that confirmed their truth. It was **fifty** years since that bit of history had left its scar on the farmer's heart; but the memory of it all rose up before him fresh and vivid as if it were but yesterday. The old man sat with outstretched head, and eyes that **were** looking far **away** beyond the wall that was opposite to him, nodding his head only as Dan'el waited for a reply.

"Iss," said the shoemaker, "they can't wake love up, 't all. But only let Truelove come along, and take it by the hand, and then sleepin' love do spring up in a minute."

"Umph!" said the farmer doubtfully, "Deth it *always*, Dan'el?"

Dan'el was rather taken aback at the question. The earnest simplicity and sadness with which it was asked brought a deeper tone of tenderness into Dan'el's words. "No, Mest' Gribble, *not always—not always*. He have come to you an' me, an' took us by the hand, an' called to us, an' hung over us, an' called us by our name—ah! the Blessed Jesus, Who is Love, to think that our love should have gone on sleepin' when He had come for to wake it! *Not always*, Mest' Gribble."

Once more the old man's thoughts were back again, intense and eager, fixed only on that of which Dan'el spoke, and again the tears gathered in his eyes as he whispered, "*Not always*, Dan'el—*not always!* Tew thenk of it!"

"But this here is true, Mest' Gribble, that if love can't wake up love, then nothin' else can." As he spoke he turned over the pages of the old well-worn Bible. "I was thinkin' about it the other day when I was reading the story back here—how Absalom wanted for to be king. He didn't tell 'em just for to blow a trumpet an' hire a score o' chaps to shout 'Long live King Absalom!' He knew well enough that folks must have more than a bit o' music an' a passle o' shoutin' before ever they'd make a king of him. So he used to get up

early in the morning and wait in the gateway o'
the city, an' when anybody came in from the country,
he would come up to 'em an' shake hands with 'em
all so friendly, an' say, 'I'm fine an' glad to see
'ee—how are 'ee then?' an' all like that. 'Where
do 'ee come from, then?—an' what do 'ee want?'
And when he'd heard all about it, he'd sigh and
look all so sad. '**Ah, if** there was only somebody
that cared for 'ee a bit, you'd be righted directly!
If I were only king—well, there!' 'I wish you
was, Sir, with all my heart,' says the man, thinkin'
that he'd never seen so nice a spoken gentleman.

"Well, he went on like that, day after day, an'
month after month, till he'd *stole the hearts o' the
men o' Israel.* Then when the day came **for to**
sound the trumpet and for **to** shout 'Absalom **is**
king'—all the folks went 'long with 'en directly,
an' word come up to David—' The hearts o' the men
o' Israel are after Absalom.'

"An' that's like 'tis with the Blessed Lord
Jesus—only that He do mean it all, instead o' only
pretendin' to. He don't send Moses 'long with a
table o' stone, an' them words cut out all sharp an'
clear in letters o' granite—*Thou shalt love the Lord
thy God with all thy* **heart.** **That isn't** enough.
We can't love only just because we are told to:
it 'll take more than that."

Farmer Gribble looked **up.** His thoughts were

back again, busied with memories of those old
times. Faces flitted past him that had been long
since in the dust. He slowly nodded his head, and
said, as if he were speaking to himself, "Yew'm
right there, tew, Dan'el. It *dew* take more than
telling tew—love dew."

Dan'el went on, never thinking for a moment
of what had so quickened the farmer's perceptions
in this matter. "So the blessed Jesus His own
self do come for to get our hearts—the altogether
lovely, full o' grace an' truth. An' if love do wake
up love, why, I wonder that the very rocks an' hills
don't cry out an' bless Him, like the hymn do say.
He, the King o' glory, a-comin' down from Heaven
a-purpose to look for you an' me, an' a-wantin' to
be our Friend, an' our Brother, an' our Saviour,
an' everything."

Dan'el stayed a moment or two as if his own
heart were feasting on it. Then he burst out again
—"O, Mest' Gribble, 't is *wonderful, wonderful*—the
love o' Jesus! I do think about it till I'm a'most lost
in wonder, love, an' praise. There, seemin' to me
that 't is just like Him—for fear that us poor folks
should think that such a glorious Lord was ever so
far above us, He is born in a stable, an' laid in a
manger; an' sometimes He is faint with hunger;
and haven't got so much as a place for to lay His
head 'pon. An' then, for fear that the fine folks

might think that **He wasn't** great enough for them,
He'll invite five thousand to dine 'long with Him
to once. An' another day He'll have angels for to
wait 'pon Him. O my blessed, blessed Lord! one
heart isn't half enough for to love Thee with.

"An' then what lovin' words do **keep** a-droppin'
from His lips. **Why,** the little children **couldn't**
help comin' up **to Him for a** blessin'; an' poor
frightened folks that was afraid o' everybody else,
came **near to** Him, they were so sure o' His love:
an' everybody that **wanted** anything felt that they
could ask Him for it in a minute. That's how He's
come for to wake up our hearts.

"Ah, an' that isn't all. All? No, the half
isn't told yet. Seemin' to me, Mest' Gribble, like
as if the Blessed Lord do come in here this morning,
an' He do say to you an' me, 'Thou art dearer to
Me than life itself—what can I do for to bless thee?'
An' my heart cries out, 'Ah! my Lord, there's my
sins.'"

"Mine tew, Dan'el,—mine tew," whispered the
farmer, very sorrowfully.

"The breakin' o' the law, an' the forgettin' God,
an' all the evil thoughts an' wishes, an' the anger
an' pride—they're dreadfully ugly to our eyes; but
He do see everything, an' do see it just as 't is, too.
Yet He do stoop over us in His love, and He do take
up our dreadful load an' suffer the curse o' the law

in our stead. If nothin' else can wake up our sleepin' love that will do it—the dreadful cry o' 'Crucify Him!' an' the dreadful hammerin' o' nails. Love do wake up an' see Him there, crowned with thorns, bleeding, torn, dyin' for me. Ah, then we can't do nothing else but love Him back again. *He loved me, and gave Himself for me.*"

Farmer Gribble sat quite still ; his chin resting on the handle of the stick, and his eyes fixed on the opposite wall, whilst the tears trickled slowly down his cheeks. He spoke very slowly—"I dew wish that I could say that, Dan'el. I dew almost believe it, tew."

"Say it," cried Dan'el, "o' course you can, Mest' Gribble. Why, you can't say anything else. Don't 'ee think that the Lord loved me an' that He passed you by. Here 't is for you an' me an' everybody."

And as he spoke he opened the Bible and pointed to the text. The old farmer took the book and laid it on his knees, whilst he rubbed his eyes and then put on his spectacles. For a few minutes he looked at the passage muttering to himself only, "*Me*—He loved *me*."

Then suddenly he looked up. "I *dew* believe it, Dan'el—to be sure I dew. He loved *me*, and gave Himself for *me*." A new light shone for a moment in the old man's face, then suddenly it was quenched again. "O, Dan'el, it be dreadful—there, to thenk

He have a-loved me like this all the days o' my life, and never got so much as a bit o' love back agen!" He shook his head in his helpless grief—"It be dreadful, dreadful!" Presently he looked up and reached out his hand to Dan'el—"I shall have hard work for to make up for lost time. Yew *wull* help me, won't yew? He dew love me; and I be a-beginnin' fur to love Him tew—an' I dew thank Him fur it."

Then kneeling down in the little place, Dan'el poured out the gladness of two hearts before the Lord.

IX

Farmer Gribble is Puzzled.

EFORE the week was over there was many another sign of the coming shower that gladdened Dan'el's heart. The meeting on the Tuesday evening found many old faces back again, whose presence there was a good sign of their "starting afresh;" whilst others came for the first time, and declared their decision to be the Lord's. And when the first meeting was over a little group of earnest inquirers remained for further direction and prayer. There—the greatest wonder to himself and to everybody else—sat Farmer Gribble. Not that he had left the parish church ; *that* never crossed his mind for a moment. Used to its forms, and with a lurking conviction still that there was some mystical superiority in its services and ministry, he could scarcely feel at home elsewhere. The only thing that marked the change was the heartiness with which he entered into the responses, almost frightening the proper old clerk, who generally had it all to himself.

But at the close of the week there came another event that made men forget all about Farmer Gribble ; they could talk of nobody else but "Diggin's."

" Diggin's," as everybody called him, was a big, brawny fellow, standing over six feet in his stockings, who had come of a family of wrestlers, and sustained the reputation of his ancestry by his physical strength and fierce combativeness. His natural wildness had found not only plenty of room for itself, but a luxuriant soil too and plenty of encouragement, as a gold digger in California. A small fortune made almost in a day had enabled him to come back to astonish his countrymen as he moved amongst them adorned with glistening rings and chain, and "loudly" attired. For a while he "lived like a lord ;" which meant that he lounged all day in the public-house, and was never so happy as when he could get up a brawl in the neighbouring market-town, and find some half-drunken fellow whom he could provoke to a fight. The small

fortune was soon squandered, and "Diggin's" had
again to take to the work of a miner, except when
in jail as a disturber of the peace. Looked upon as
a sort of hero by the young fellows of the place,
Dan'el had often grieved over his influence, and
had once or twice spoken plain words of warning to
him but only to evoke a terrible volley of oaths.

One evening as Dan'el talked with Cap'n Joe,
the conversation turned on the subject of "Diggin's"
and his latest mischief. "Well, Dan'el, there is
one cure for him, and only one. We must try that,
I think," said the Cap'n. "The Lord can bring
him down, an' make him so much of a blessing as
he has been a curse."

Dan'el looked up from his work and pursed his
mouth for a few seconds, then nodded his head
slowly. "So He can, Cap'n Joe; so He can. O'
course He can." And Dan'el nodded his head more
vigorously : "Knock him down in a minute. Why,
come for to think of it now, I do expect that David
was fine an' glad for to get hold o' that great
Goliath o' Gath, for when *he* was killed the rest o'
them would see that there wasn't a bit o' chance
for any o' them little ones, an' they'd give in
directly." The notion quite delighted Dan'el; and
after thinking of it again for a minute or two, he
nodded his head as if it were a settled thing. "We
must agree together about it, Cap'n, and then stick

to it. Why, bless His name, 't would be all the
more to His glory to bring down a great sinner like
that, an' nobody could despair o' His mercy then.
That's it, Cap'n Joe : we must shake hands over
that."

They shook hands accordingly, Dan'el shaking
his head at the same time ; and from that day forward for many months each of them pleaded with
God on this man's behalf. But "Diggin's" for his
part, might have known of their agreement. He
became wilder and more reckless than ever, and
seemed to take a special delight in shouting his
oaths when Dan'el or Cap'n Joe was in hearing.
But still they pleaded on, confident in the power
and promise of the Lord.

This week the answer came ; in a way that
stirred all Penwinnin. It was on the Saturday, just
as the men were leaving their work underground.
All indeed had gone but "Diggin's," and he had
picked up his tools, and now stood for a moment
trimming his candle, moving the soft clay with
which it was stuck in his hard round hat, so that it
might have room to burn.

A weird sight was it down there in the deep
darkness, as the small circle of candle-light fell on
the figure of the miner in his flannel dress, stained
a dull ochreish red by the mine water. It lit up the
face, not ill-looking by any means, and it touched

the jet-black hair. It showed the broad shoulders and the upper part of the stalwart frame. Then the thick darkness gathered on every side, except on the glistening roof close overhead; there the light flung a huge shadow, hanging over the miner like some horrible spirit that belonged to those lonely depths of gloom.

The others had already reached the shaft, and were now some distance up the ladders that led to the surface. Placing the candle again in front of his hat, "Diggin's" hastily shouldered his tools and was just going to hurry after his companions when suddenly a voice called him. It was not the voice of any one who worked there; it called him, too, by a name that he had not heard since he was a happy little lad at his mother's side.

"*Mat! Mat!*" cried the voice very earnestly, and with such tenderness as he had not heard for years, "*Come back, Mat! come back!*"

The strangeness of the call, the voice, the name, all startled him. Taking the candle from his hat again, he turned round and held it before him with one hand, whilst with the other he shaded his eyes, and looked away into the gloom from whence the sound had come.

Again the voice called, louder and nearer this time, and with greater entreaty: "*Come back, Mat —quick! quick!*"

It seemed so close that at once he hastened on a few paces, expecting to see some one.

"Who is it?" he cried. But his voice only went echoing in the dismal windings, waking up the far-off hollow caverns. Again he called, "Who is it? Where are you?" and leaning forward he strained his ear to catch some answer in the rumbling echo. Then suddenly, with awful crash of thunder, a huge mass of rock fell on the spot where he had been standing but a minute before.

Crouching against the wall of the passage, he expected at first that the loosened stones overhead would fall in and bury him. Then assured of safety, he came to see what hope the fallen rock had left of his getting out. The way was completely blocked, and it was plain at once that he could not escape until help should come from the other side. As he stood there he caught sight of the pick that he had dropped when the voice startled him. He stooped to take it up, but lifted only the splintered handle; the rest of it was buried under the rock. Then it suddenly flashed upon him: the peril he had been in, the meaning of the voice and all the strange deliverance.

He leaned against the rock with a deep groan. "A minute later and I should have been in hell!" he muttered to himself—"in *hell!*"

He sat down quite overcome and almost faint, and buried his face in his hands. "In hell!" he

Y

whispered again, as if slowly realizing its terribleness. Then he looked up suddenly. "Why didn't I go there?" he asked aloud, awed and staring into the darkness as if some one stood there listening. A dozen echoes flung back the words; then they died in the hollow distance.

"Nobody ever did more to deserve it—nobody!" he went on in the same tone. "*Nobody*," rang back the echoes. Then his voice sank to a whisper. "*And yet He spared me!*"

The candle threw the shadow of the hat over his face and hid it; but the light fell on the hands as they hung down helplessly before him. And the tears that came trickling out of the darkness shone and sparkled in the light before they reached the ground.

"He spared *me!*" he whispered to himself again and again: "*me*. And after all that I done against Him, too! Me!" And the tears fell more quickly. "I *do* wish that I could kneel and thank Him for it. But there, I shall never be fit for that my own self: leastways not for years. No, 't isn't for me to speak to Him at all, after blasphemin' and grievin' Him like I have done." And again he leaned forward and buried his face in his hands.

That he should get out again was a matter of which he had not a moment's doubt. It was nothing to him that he might perhaps remain for many hours before any one would know of what had happened; or that perhaps, so much of the ground had fallen that it would take some two or three days before they could rescue him. The deliverance was so strange, so wonderful, and for such an one as he! it could not be that he should just die there after all. That did not once occur to him.

"If I could only thank Him for it! only tell Him how sorry I am that I've been so wicked! To spare *me* like that!" Then his thoughts turned to the voice that had called him and its tenderness. It seemed to ring again in his ears, "Mat! Mat!" It certainly was his mother's voice: nobody else ever called him by that name; if they did, nobody else could speak it like that. There rose before the miner many memories of her, no one of which he could ever recall in his wildest moments without a softening restraint. Many a strange, almost mad freak of generosity had lit up the darkness of his life in a way which nothing but that memory could ever explain. How often she had taken him by the hand, and kneeling down together had prayed for him, and taught him to pray. As he thought of it now he looked up suddenly. "Perhaps He will let me thank Him for mother's sake," he whispered to himself timidly. And he was about to kneel and speak to his mother's God. But he checked himself directly. That holy mother was so far away and so different from himself. Again the evil of his life rushed on his mind and smote him dumb. Then with the bitter sense of his badness almost breaking his heart, he sat down again, his hands hanging in dreary helplessness, and the tears creeping heavily down his cheeks.

So he sat without moving and without a word; the burden of his wasted and wicked life growing in its weight of misery. The candle flickered, and after struggling bravely to shine on, it went out, leaving him in that dreadful darkness. But he sat on almost unconscious of the change, able to think of nothing else but those evil memories that pressed upon him.

Meanwhile the other miners had heard the noise of the falling rock, and knowing that their companion was behind, had hastened down again, only to find the way completely blocked. It was just possible that he had noticed the loosening rock and had escaped on the other side, but not one of them had any hope of it. At once they set to work to dig through the fallen mass, working silently, and dreading lest each stone they turned should reveal the dead body. Meanwhile Michael Treleaven, the oldest amongst them, had climbed up with the tidings of the accident, having arranged to get round to the other side through some disused workings that he remembered in another part of the mine.

" He isn't killed," said young Cap'n Joe, as he
heard of it, and got ready at once to go down in
search of him. " He isn't killed."

But the grave old Michael shook his head.
" ' Diggin's ' have been often reproved, Cap'n Joe;
an' he have a-hardened his neck. 'Pend 'pon it,
comrades, his time is come, an' a terrible judgment
'tis too; ' suddenly destroyed, an' that wethout
remedy,' as the Book do say."

For an hour or more " Diggin's " had been sitting in the lonely darkness, when suddenly he heard
a faint splash away in the hollow workings. He
listened for a moment wondering. " Only another
bit o' rock fallin' away," he whispered to himself,
and turned again to his sorrowful thoughts. Presently there came again the sound of the splashing
as if some one were moving through the water, and
a rumbling noise as of voices away there. Cool and
almost ignorant of fear as he was generally, the
strange deliverance, the mysterious voice that had
called him, the long loneliness in the dark, and now
these unaccountable noises, all unnerved him.
Horrid fancies began to shape themselves in his
mind; dreadful stories crowded in upon him, chill-
ing his blood with icy terror. Then came a
moment's flash of light, and again the voices rumbling frightfully about the place, ending in a shout
that rolled along the hollow passages like thunder.

A minute later, and out of the darkness appeared the familiar presence of young Cap'n Joe, and his cheery voice rang: "Diggin's! Diggin's! Are you safe?"

But surely that was not "Diggin's" voice that replied so mournfully · "Aw, Cap'n Joe; come here, come here!"

"There, I knew it," said old Michael solemnly. "Cut off without remedy."

For a moment Cap'n Joe's confidence failed him. Thinking that the others had dug through, from that side, and had found the mangled body, he hastened forward, ready for anything except that which met him. There sat "Diggin's," not so much as lifting his face to the light.

"Cap'n Joe," he whispered hoarsely, "I'm fine and glad that you're come. He have spared me— *me!* An' after all that I've a-been, too! A minute more an' I should have been in hell! I can't stir till you do kneel down an' thank Him. An' you, too, Michael,—do'ee. I been wantin' to, but I can't speak His name with my lips." Then the voice was choked in grief.

The three kneeled together there, and gave thanks to God. Young Cap'n Joe triumphantly, and with a ringing confidence that this deliverance was not to end here. But old Michael Treleaven was solemn, almost severe: "Diggin's have de-

served Thy judgments, Lord; let Thy sparing
goodness lead him to repentance. Thou hast plucked
him from the jaws o' hell. May it be a warnin' to
him. Snatch him as a brand from the burnin' !
Take him up out o' the horrible pit ! ' "

An eager crowd waited about the mouth of the
shaft. Those who stood at the edge of it looking
down into the gloom saw the glimmer of a light.
" They are comin'," went amongst the crowd, and
a great silence settled on all. Then far below they
could faintly discern the candle, moving upwards,
and at once there came a shout from old Michael,
" He's safe, comrades ! "

" Thank God ! " said every one, devoutly.
Then old Michael stepped off the ladder, and told
the story of " Diggin's " escape. And almost
before the old man had done, " Diggin's " himself
came up, only looking about him sorrowfully as the
people fell back to make room for him. And close
behind came young Cap'n Joe.

The impressions of his deliverance did not leave
Mat when he got into the daylight again; they
deepened. Such goodness to such an one as he
was overwhelmed him. And by the side of it rose
up the memory of his sins, so burdening him that he
could scarcely touch his food, or even work or sleep.
At times he roared in the disquietude of his soul.
What David sang of and Bunyan pictured, he passed

through. In vain he heard the Gospel promises: they were for everybody but himself. Neither Dan'el nor young Cap'n Joe could help him. There was no light, no peace, no hope for him.

So three weeks had gone by, and Mat, as everybody called him now, was sitting on the Sunday morning in the little chapel at Penwinnin. The Preacher was quietly going on in a somewhat drowsy way, when suddenly the congregation were startled: without a sign of what was coming, Mat leapt from his seat high into the air, and clasping his hands, gave a shout that seemed to shake the place. "Hallelujah!" he cried again and again.

Deliverance had come. The prison doors were opened and his chains were loosed, and now he literally danced for joy. The Father had welcomed him with the kiss of forgiveness, with the best robe, and the ring for the finger, and shoes for the feet; now what else could he do but begin to be merry?

"I can praise Thee now, my Lord, and I will," he cried, as the place rang again. The Preacher, a quiet, argumentative brother, stopped and looked over the high pulpit. Then he coughed, bewildered. The joy spread through the congregation until a score of voices rang with loud thanksgiving. The power of the Lord was present to heal, and others who had gone sorrowing for many days found joy and peace in believing. The service was turned

into an inquiry meeting, and anxious seekers stayed on hour after hour, so that the chapel could not be closed until late at night. Each evening of the week meetings were held, and scores came under the influence of the Power, that transformed them as completely as it did the Californian Mat.

To poor Farmer Gribble all this was not only perplexing, it was outrageous. Some of his prejudices had begun to soften, but on that Sunday morning they all shot up again, as he found himself suddenly in the midst of a Cornish revival. The short hair bristled over his head; the colour flew to his cheeks. At last he rose up and hurried from the place, hurt and angry, determined that he would have nothing more to do with a people who could tolerate such proceedings.

It was with an almost triumphant air of relief that he turned into the hallowed stillness of the old parish church, that afternoon. Its holy quiet was sweet and refreshing, as when one steps from the fierce glare of noon into cold depths of leafy shade. But as the farmer kneeled in prayer before the service began, he had forgotten all about church, or chapel either. He only wanted to love that gracious Lord Whom he had grieved so long, and with this one thought filling heart and mind, he stood up at the beginning of the Liturgy. The words were no more a dead letter to him, but the utterance of his innermost heart; and tears filled his eyes and his voice was choked more than once as he thought of that loving Lord, and joined in confessing: *We have erred, and strayed from Thy ways like lost sheep.* Farmer Gribble could not sing; but to-day he almost put the old clerk out in trying to, for he wanted to find some outlet for the blessedness that he felt in the words: *Thou art the King of Glory, O Christ; Thou art the everlasting Son of the Father. . . . When Thou hadst overcome the sharpness of death, Thou didst open the kingdom of heaven to all believers.* He would have been startled if he had heard the old clerk's growl when the service was done: "That there Mest' Gribble es wuss than the Methodis' their awn selves, a-goin' on so an' a-puttin' anybody out like that. He ought to be 'shamed of hisself; iss, he ought. Why don't he go to chapel an' keep there?"

Next day the farmer came, full of complaint, to his old friend Dan'el. "Lewk yere, Dan'el," he began, the indignation flashing up again for a moment—"lewk yere. I can't make mun out for the life o' me. What be all thes yere noise about? Ef these yere chaps be right, then I be all wrang still, but I can't go on like that theare, an' I doan't mane tew, nayther."

"Well, Mest' Gribble, don't then; nobody wants 'ee to," said Dan'el, playfully.

"But I can't abide it, Dan'el. And they haven't a-got no bezness for tew be goin' on like it, an'—"

"Stop, stop, friend," cried Dan'el, gently, seeing that the farmer was getting warm. "Don't let you an' me go a-talkin' so. The Lord have got different ways o' comin' to different people. He do come to some with a star for a token; an' never a sound in the still night, but that there gentle shinin' a-leadin' 'em on an' on to the Blessed Jesus. Then they fall down an' worship Him, and open their treasures o' gold, an' myrrh, an' frankincense. But they are the *wise* men, Mest' Gribble; and because they are wise they won't go quarrellin' with the shepherds if the Lord do choose to come to them with a great light that do frighten 'em a'most out o' their wits, an' because they do go glorifyin' God."

"But, Dan'el, yew don't mean fur tew zay that they went shoutin' an' jumpin' about like a passle o' mazed volks, dew 'ee?" said the farmer, gently, for all the indignation had died out of his words now.

"Well, I expect some o' them did. You see it do all depend 'pon the sort o' men, Mest' Gribble. People would never be so foolish as to go talkin' like this about anything else. They'd leave room for different sorts o' folks to show their feelin's in different sorts o' ways. S'pose now some old uncle died an' left you a thousand pounds. You do get the letter to-morrow mornin' tellin' 'ee of it. An'

Mat, he do get a letter sayin' the same thing—there's a thousand pounds left for him too. Why, he'd only stop to read the letter half through, then he would jump up an' run off to tell one an' another; he'd shout an' clap his hands an' go on so! I s'pose that you would put the letter in the fire, wouldn't 'ee? 'Aw,' you'd say, 'it can't be true 't all, for I can't jump about like that, an' I don't mean to, neither.'"

Dan'el paused a moment, and looked up for the farmer's reply. "Yew'm right, Dan'el—quite right," said Mest' Gribble, slowly noddin' his head over the handle of his walking-stick.

"No. You'd read that letter over half a dozen times, Mest' Gribble, for to make sure of it; and then you'd put it in your pocket without sayin' a word to anybody, an' you'd go right off for to see the will, an' think o' the best thing to do with it. That's what you'd do, isn't it?"

Mest' Gribble nodded his head.

"But you'd have the money so much as Mat would. An' Mat would have it so much as you, every bit."

Slowly the farmer rose. "I will go home an' look to the Will, Dan'el." Then he held out his hand with a sigh. "Yew must teach me, please. I be so ignorant as a child, an' obstinate tew— dreadful obstinate. Good-bye, an' thank 'ee, Dan'el, thank 'ee."

X.

Dan'el's Notions about Grumbling.

T was a dull November evening, damp and close. A dense mist had hung about the hills all day and crept heavily along the valleys; now it had come filling the room. The fire sulked half asleep in the little grate, waking up sometimes only to blink uncomfortably, and sink to sleep again. Altogether, so far as the weather was concerned, it seemed a good deal easier to grumble at other people for grumbling than to talk about it in any bright and happy fashion. But plainly Dan'el had made up his mind not to be beaten by that

There was almost a defiant cheeriness about the
way in which he gave out the hymn :

"Come, friends, the Lord tune our hearts.   Ten's
an' 'levens.

> 'O Heavenly King, Look down from above !
> Assist us to sing Thy mercy and love :
> So sweetly o'erflowing, So plenteous the store,
> Thou still art bestowing, And giving us more.' "

By the time they had got to the end of the first
verse the dulness had begun to lift from some
hearts, and before the hymn was done all was
glowing and joyful.   Dan'el's prayer completed the
gladness; so *real*, so hearty, with such a triumph in
the Lord Jesus, that it was irresistible.   All rose
ready to enter thoroughly into the subject that had
been previously announced for the evening.   Yet
there was, perhaps, one exception ; but only one.
Widow Pascoe sat and sighed with a kind of obstinate dolefulness, as if she had set herself to be the
witness of her creed, according to which grumbling
was one of the truest signs of grace.

Dan'el opened the Bible at the First Epistle to
the Corinthians, the tenth chapter.   The sturdy
forefinger guided his eye to the tenth verse.   But
the misty light was too dim for his failing sight.
In vain the spectacles were drawn to the tip of the
nose, whilst the head was thrust backward for a
more distant view.   But it was all of no avail.

"Here, Cap'n Joe, you must take an' read it for me, please ; 't is to the tenth verse."

"Neither murmur ye," Cap'n Joe began, in his ringing bass voice.

"But stop a minute," Dan'el interrupted, "seemin' to me that we ought to begin further up than that. What's that about *neither be ye idolaters ?*"

"In the seventh verse?" And Cap'n Joe read on : "*Neither be ye idolaters, as were some of them ; as it is written, The people sat down to eat and drink and rose up to play.*"

"There," cried Dan'el, looking up suddenly, "that's what I wanted. You see the Lord doesn't only give us a commandment not to grumble, but He puts it alongside o' all the dreadfulest things in the world. An' I want for all of us to look at that, for grumblers be like to us old folks—they can only see plain when things are a goodish way off. Their own faults an' failin's are too close for 'em to notice; but they have got a wonderful quick eye, sure 'nough, for the faults o' their neighbours, an' a quick tongue for to tell about 'em, too. So now, friend grumbler, as you can't see yourself, look 'pon your company, for they say that a man is known by his friends. Here is a shockin' set for a man to be in, specially if he do count hisself a Christian. Why, this here murmurin' have joined 'ee to idolaters. You're a-keepin' company with shameless

people. You're goin' along hand in hand with
them that do tempt Christ. There's pretty company for anybody, isn't it ? "

Dan'el stayed a moment, as if this needed time to
sink in.   It was evident that to Widow Pascoe it was
new light, and gave her "quite a turn ; " for there
were two things that she prided herself upon : one
was the expansive whiteness of her widow's cap,
the other was the very select set that she admitted
to her friendship.

Before she had time to recover, Dan'el went on
again : "An' it is n't just a bit o' chance like either,
findin' the grumblers here.   A good man may sometimes be jostled by an ill crowd ; but this is where
the grumbler do belong ; 't is his proper place.
There's a dreadful picture in this Book where the
King o' glory is comin' for to punish His enemies
—comin' with ten thousand of His saints for to
take vengeance 'pon the rebels.   Ah, folks will
stare then.   Here the angels are takin' hold o' one
an' another.   Why, they have made a mistake, surely!
The King o' glory is come ' to execute judgment '
'pon drunkards an' thieves an' liars ; but that man
is a sort o' religious gentleman ; an' that woman is
very religious sometimes !   But the angels bind
'em hand an' foot accordin' to orders.   Read out
the proclamation, Cap'n Joe, will 'ee, please ?   'T is
in Jude-the fourteenth verse, I reckon."

Slowly and solemnly the words fell from Cap'n Joe's lips; *" Behold, the Lord cometh with ten thousands of His saints, to execute judgment upon all, and to convince all that are ungodly among them of all their ungodly deeds which they have ungodly committed, and of all their hard speeches which ungodly sinners have spoken against Him. These are murmurers, complainers."*

" Ah, there 't is, friends; there 't is !" cried Dan'el. "' These are *murmurers, complainers.'* First and foremost among the rebels stand their names : MURMURERS ! COMPLAINERS ! "

Widow Pascoe started slightly.

" But finish it, Cap'n Joe, will 'ee, please ? "

" Murmurers, complainers, walking after their own lusts ; and their mouth speaketh great swelling words, having men's persons in admiration because of advantage."

Then Dan'el broke in again : " Not 'zackly the worst kind o' grumblers either ; for you see they *could* speak a work o' praise sometimes, when there was something to be got by it. But 't is busy-all for to get anything else but grumblin' out o' the grumblers that be goin' now-a-days."

Again Daniel stayed a few moments, as if that needed time " for to get well home," as he called it. Then he went on more cheerily :

' But mind, friends, there's some things that

anybody may grumble against without much harm.
He may grumble at his own sin an' folly, an' be
none the worse for it, 'specially if he'll set to work
for to mend so well as murmur. There's things that
a man can't help grumblin' about if there's any soul
in him at all. The man who can see a great evil,
an' hold his tongue about it is every bit so bad as he
that do hinder good by grumbliu' at it. They two
can set up business with the same stock in trade.

"An' there's another thing, too, that I don't
want for to forget. There's a little bit more excuse
for some folks grumblin' than there is for others.
When anybody have got all that he ought to wish
for an' yet do go grumblin', I'd give him this here
physic so strong and so bitter as ever I could. But
poor folks that have got to grind day an' night for
to keep the wolf from the door, and poor women
that are weak to begin with, an' got to go carryin'
a great pack o' worries 'pon their backs,—well, I'm
sure my Master would like me for to sweeten the
physic a bit for them, an' flavour it up like they do
for the children. Yet, you poor worried folks, don't
'e go a-thinkin' that cares and worries will excuse
your grumblin'; they won't do that 't all. 'T is
put down for you so much as for anybody : '*Neither
murmur ye.*' "

Dan'el's words and tones grew full of an exquisite pathos and tenderness as he went on :

" You do want more help than some folks do, an'
you shall have it too.   I was thinkin' about it down
by the sea the other day.   When the tide come in
it filled up the great caves so easy every bit as it
did the little holes in the rocks.   Great wants is
only like plenty o' room for the help o' the Blessed
Jesus.   Why, if there hadn't been any lame folks
an' sick folks an' blind folks when He was down
here 'pon earth He could never have let people see
how merciful He was.   An' so 't is you that have
got most for to bear, and most for to carry, that do
come to know how kind an' lovin' He is.   Bless
His dear name, He do keep such lovely little bits o'
tenderness for us when we're cast down an' tired;
an' He do take up the great heaps o' care an' carry
'em for us.   No, you poor dears that are tempted
an' tried mustn't go a-grumblin', because you've got
such a glorious Lord waitin' for to help 'ee, you
have.   An' don't go thinkin' that they that have
got everything haven't got any worries 'long with
it.   There was one of our Preachers once, he lent
me an old book called *The Christian Jewel of Contentment.*   There was a lot o' capital things in it,
and this was amongst 'em : ' The devil is called,
in the Bible, *Beel-zebub ;* that do mean " the god o'
flies " ; an' you're sure to find 'em a-buzzin' about
the honey pots o' prosperity.'

" But come, friends, we must go a bit deeper

into this matter, an' track this old varmint right up to his den. I don't wonder that the Lord punished it like He did. 'T is just what the Book do say, such a provokin' kind of thing : so aggravatin' an' so insultin'. Here is the lovin' Father carin' for us, an' arrangin' for our good an' blessin' us, all so kind an' so wise. An' all the time here's a silly blind man who can't see any o' the evil that the Lord is a-keepin' him out of, nor half o' the good that He is a-leadin' him into; and yet he's a-mutterin' an' a-murmurin' just like as if things was put together a-purpose for to spite him. 'T is dreadful, sure 'nough !—dreadful.

"I'm quite sure o' one thing, that this here grumblin' is the devil's oldest son; an' the image of his father, too. He do always claim his place, an' go first, an' after 'en do come all the rest o' his rabble an' crew. Some say that Adam and Eve fell through pride, an' some do put it down to other things; but 't was old Discontent—he was to the bottom o' all the mischief. 'Nonsense,' he grumbled, 'nonsense, Eve, don't you think that you are blest 't all. You never will be till you've tasted that there apple.' So 't was long with Cain : if he hadn't murmured first, he wouldn't have murdered afterwards. 'T is a ghastly old thing is this Grumblin', friends; don't let us have anything to do with it. Why, back here in the history of Israel there's thousands an' thousands o' graves, an' for every one o' them there's the same thing put up on the tombstone : *Here lies a man that died for grumblin'.* Ah ! that was mightier than Pharaoh and all his chariots, for they escaped him. That was worse than slavery, for God could fetch them out o' that. It was worse than all their enemies put together—grumblin' killed them !

"An' yet there's scores o 'good people who count that grumblin' is no sin at all. They'll confess their sins, and they'll own to unbelief an' scores o' things. But they never thought o' kneeling down an' sayin': *O Lord, forgive my grumblin', and help me never to do it again, for Jesus Christ's sake. Amen.* Yet we do need to, friends. I'm sure we do need to. Grumblin' have been the death o' thousands; and if we don't take care it will be the death of us too.

"But there, it won't do for me to have all the talkin'. Come, Cap'n Joe, what have you got to say about it ? You aren't no friend to it, I do know."

"Well," said Cap'n Joe, "I've been turning over in my mind what you said about this grumbling being so aggravating and insulting. So it is. I was thinking, suppose that we were lost among a savage people, our very lives in danger and a great price demanded for our freedom; then there comes One, and out of pure love and pity He gives Himself up to be plundered and stripped for our deliverance. Now He comes to us with all His bleeding wounds

and marks of ill-treatment, and He says, 'Follow
Me. I will bring you safely to the Father's House.
I will guide you. I have arranged for the supply
of all your wants. I am able to protect you from
all enemies. Follow Me!' Our hearts are full of
love to Him; and thankful and trustful we set out.
But soon there comes a bit of a hill and He hears
us grumbling because 't isn't level ground. He
leads us through the forest, and we grumble at the
brambles. Ah! I think I see Him look round
upon us so hurt and so grieved. No enemy could
ever hurt Him like that. After all His love and
promises, all that He has done for us and all that
He is going to do, to go fretting and grumbling; it
is a ghastly sin, as you do say, dear leader."

"And to treat *Him* like that, friends—the
Blessed Lord Jesus!" and as Dan'el spoke the
tears trickled down his face. 'But go on, Cap'n
Joe; an' I'm glad to hear 'ee, too."

"Well, there was only one thing more that I
thought of: 't is such a shameful forgetting of the
past. These grumbling Israelites forgot all about
the brick kiln and the burning sun, and the task-
master's whip and the drowned children. And
they forgot all about the great deliverance: how
they had come over the Red Sea, and how God had
fed them with the manna."

"'Zackly," cried Dan'el, his eye twinkling

merrily, and his face lit up, " 'zackly, Cap'n Joe.
'T is always like that with this here Grumblin'.
I thought about it the other day when I met the
Coastguardman 'pon the cliffs. 'Well, friend,' I
said, ' you are like Thankfulness.' ' How so, Dan'el?'
says he. ' Well,' I said, ' that walks along 'pon top
o' the cliffs with a telescope under his arm; an' he
spies out the Goodness of God all around. He has
his eye 'pon the blessin' that is ever so far off,
keepin' it in mind; an' he sees the mercy that is
only just turnin' the corner. That's Thankfulness,
lookin' far an' near, findin' mercies everywhere.'
' Ah, Dan'el, I wish I was more like that ! ' says he.
' Iss,' I said, ' an' I wish I was too, for 't is a brave
deal better than bein' like poor old Grumblin'. He
haven't got a spy-glass at all, nor nothin' o' the sort.
All he has got is a sort o' magnifyin'-glass, and
every little worry he can find he do put under that,
an' make it look so big that he do come to think
that there isn't anything else in all the world."

Farmer Gribble looked around in the silence
that followed, and then began in his slow and almost
drawling way; yet in his tone and manner, and in
everything about him, there was a childlike simplicity that was very beautiful. " Well, Dan'el, I
be feared that I can't say nowt fur tew dew anybody any gude. I dew wish I could. And I ought
tew, tew; for I've gone grumblin' for these years

an' years; and I've a-heerd mun say, 'Set a thief
tew catch a thief.' But I dew thenk the Lord, I
heven't so much as feeled fur tew want tew grumble
fur thes long while now. And I dew count that a
taste of the love of Jesus be a sure and certain cure
fur grumblin'. He 'th made it all so different;
why theare, 'tes no gude tryin' fur tew help it. I
be forced to go praisin' Him all the day drough, an'
I heven't so much as a breath left fur tew grumble
weth ef I wanted tew. And I *dew* thank Him fur
it weth all my heart; *that* I dew.'

Dan'el listened with delight, nodding his head
as each sentence came slowly unfolding itself. To
see the discontented and grumpy Mest' Gribble
turned into this, was really something to rejoice over;
and such joy came welling up in his soul that Dan'el
took the Hymn-Book as a relief. Come, friends, we
must sing a verse or two :

> ' Long as I live beneath,
>   To Thee O let me live !
> To Thee my every breath
>   In thanks and praises give !
> Whate'er I have, whate'er I am,
> Shall magnify my Maker's name.

> 'My soul and all its powers,
>   Thine, wholly Thine, shall be ;
> All, all my happy hours
>   I consecrate to Thee :
> Me to Thine image now restore,
> And I shall praise Thee evermore.'

"Now, friends," Dan'el began as they settled down again, "I've got one or two things more that I do want to say, an' I'll try and be quick over it, too." Putting on his spectacles he drew from his pocket a bulky pocket-book, and found a page that was carefully turned down. "Here is a bit that I got from that old book; 't is uncommon good."

Stumbling a little over the large, straggling hand-writing, Dan'el read : "*It tokeneth a man of very ill-nature when the prick of a pin maketh the flesh to rankle and fester. So it is the sign of a corrupt soul when every little trouble and affliction maketh a man break out into frettings and grumbles. The wound would be nothing but for the murmuring spirit.*"* Then Dan'el tightened his lips and nodded his head.

"There's a text for a sermon there, friends; only I mustn't stay to preach it now. I wish folks would believe it : 't isn't their worries that set 'em grumbling ; 't is their own teasy an' fretful souls.

"An' then this grumblin' is such a catchin' kind o' a thing. The old lion walketh about seeking whom he may devour. But there's one thing that's worse than the roaring lion—that's the bad sheep that goes spreadin' mischief all among the flock.

---

* *The Rare Jewel of Christian Contentment.* By Jeremiah Burroughs. London, 1652. Dan'el quoted the substance of the sentence, but not the exact words.

Ah, that's the grumbler! He goes about poisonin'
everybody. No wonder that he was 'destroyed of
the destroyer,' as the Book do say. I can mind
hearin' years ago about an old sea-captain back in
the old fightin' times: the brave old fellow, he used
to say that, by God's help, he wasn't afraid o'
Frenchmen or o' storms, but for a grumbler there
was no cure except the yard-arm.

"Well, dear friends, as Mest' Gribble do say,
a taste o' the love o' Jesus is a sure cure for
grumblin'. For that, as for everything else, we
must get away to the Cross o' the Blessed Saviour.
Ah! when we do get a sight o' His sufferin' for us,
that makes our sufferin' too light for to grumble
about it. Only let us see Him stripped o' everything, mocked an' beaten an' crucified for our
sakes—and yet *He opened not His mouth!* Ah,
bless His holy name, that takes all the grumblin'
out of us: turns it right round into love an' praise.
Only get away to Calvary and live in sight o' the
Cross, friends, an' we shan't any of us have a breath
left for to grumble with. But come, there's five
minutes more if anybody else has got a word for
to say."

"Mat," as he was called now—the Californian
"Diggin's" of old days,—sat, scarcely able to
restrain himself. His heart glowed still with its
"first love": the joy of God's salvation had rather

deepened since that memorable Sunday morning than grown less.

"Come, Mat, you've want to speak a bit, I see," said Dan'el.

In a moment Mat sprang up, his eyes streaming with tears, and his whole frame heaving with excitement. "I been tryin' to be quiet, but I can't. Grumblin'! Aw, I been thinkin' about it while I been sittin' here. We've been an' got ourselves into trouble, an' now we're sent off to jail for it. We grumble agen the treadmill; 't is such hard work. An' we grumble because we can't get more to eat. And the jailer do say : ' Iss, you should ha' thought o' that before, an' should ha' kept out o' the place; 't is all along o' your own doin's.' But to think of it, friends! to have the King o' Glory comin' down to take *my* place, an' to bear *my* punishment, an' then comin' to *me* with a free pardon! To have the Father's arms about my neck, an' His love ringin' in my soul, all the day long! Hallelujah!" And the little room rang with the shout.

XI

Dan'el's Advice to the Beginners.

BESIDES Farmer Gribble and Mat, many another new comer had found his way to the little company, until the room at Thomas Toms' was scarcely large enough for those who crowded into it. It was for these that Dan'el had chosen the subject of this evening.

"I want for to say a few plain things to you that are young in the way. It won't do us old ones any harm either, for we have all o' us got an uncommon love for stickin' just inside o' the wicket-gate, like as if religion was nothin' but standin' still when once you're through that. An' I should be glad if you young ones would please to write down the rules that I'm goin' to give 'e, an' keep them where you can see them three or four times a day. That would do us old folks good, too; but old folks 'll listen to good advice, only they've got out o' the way o' takin' it, somehow.

"Well, now, the first Rule is this—*Be sure that you're in the right road.* Put that down. You'll never get along at all if you do keep stoppin' and wonderin' whether 'tis the right road. I was preachin' over to Stithians the other day, an' comin' home I lost myself—or thought I did. Ah, 'twas poor speed with me then. I was afraid that I should have to go back again, an' so I went on at a snail's pace. Well, I came to a directin' post, but 'twas all weather-beaten an' worn, and it didn't help me a bit. 'Poor preacher you be, then,' I says. Very soon I saw a man comin'. 'This the way to Penwinnin?' I called out. 'Iss, straight on.' Ah, I was off then, so fast as I could get over the ground. You'll never get on till you're quite sure that you are in the right road.

"Why, there was John Wesley his own self—he was hurryin' about all the days o' his life, but he never got any forwarder with it all; 'twas nothin' but forth an' back, forth an' back, like the door 'pon the hinges, till he got right hold o' them

words—*The Son of God loved me and gave Himself
for me*. Then away he went, an' never so much as
looked back again. Now, you beginners, do 'e get
into a way o' restin' 'pon Jesus without any doubt.
Don't ever go tryin' to be content with good
feelin's an' good desires an' good resolutions. They
are all very well, an' thank God for them; but
good feelin's is turned into bad failin's when we
put our trust in them. Do get into a way o'
lookin' straight up to the Cross for salvation—
mornin', noon, an' night. Bright or dull, glad or
sad, there it is for us always, *in Him we have re-
demption through His blood, even the forgiveness of
sins*. Ah, the Devil do keep thousands o' people
in prison all their days. 'Come,' he do say,
'come—you aren't so happy as you used to be; or
you aren't so happy as you ought to be. You must
come to jail.' An' there he keeps 'em, lettin' 'em
out o' the cage once in a while for a bit o' fresh
air when 'tis oncommon fine weather. And all the
time the Blessed Lord Jesus has finished the work
for every one o' us. Why, there's times when I've
got to buckle them words about me like a life-belt—
He loved me and gave Himself for me. When my good
feelin's an' my good everything else is clean swept
away, an' I must hang on to the promise. Bless the
Lord, I can always get safe to land again with that."

Farmer Gribble's face was quite a picture as he

sat listening. Like Naaman when he was healed, and his flesh was as the flesh of *a little child,* so it seemed with him. The hard lines of his face were softened wonderfully, and the blustering man had changed to a child-like simplicity and humbleness. There with his chin resting on his stick, his face beaming with joy, he muttered the words to himself, that he claimed now as his very own—"*He loved me and gave Himself for me.*"

"So that is rule one," Daniel went on again. "And now for rule two.

"*Don't go thinkin' that the Road to Heaven is all up-hill.*

"There's a good many things—it do take all the patience I've got for to stand 'em. But there's one thing I *can't* abide, an' don't want to either. I can't abide to hear people go talkin' brave an' cheerful about everything in the world except religion ; *that's* always doleful an' dismal an' wisht. They can put a bit o' cheerfulness into their work, an' stick to that. But begin with religion—they'll groan directly. The man can do his ten hours, an' more than that to a pinch ; an' the woman can manage the washin', an' look after the baby, an' cook the dinner too, and not think that 'tis anything very dreadful. But when 'tis in the Lord's service—listen to 'em then. They *are* such poor, weak creatures ; an' they *have* got

so *many* troubles, an' so *many* trials, an' so *many*
temptations; an' they *are* so full o' their doubts an'
their fears; an' the devil he *is* so busy. That's it;
that's it.   Smart enough, an' strong enough, an'
clever enough for everything else in the world—
except the one thing that they was made for, *servin'*
the Lord!   I can't abide it.   Don't any o' you
young folks get into such ghastly ways, for pity's
sake.   You *are* poor, weak creatures,—o' course you
are; an' sayin' so a hundred times a day won't
make 'e any stronger.   You've got temptations
an' trials—o' course you have, an' groanin' over
them 'll only make 'em look more an' bigger.   But
what else have we got?   Ah, folks stop there, an'
that's how they fail."

Then the hasty, impatient voice passed into such
tenderness that it touched every heart.

"Don't get into a way o' lookin' always upon
that side, like as if that's all.   Ah, bless His name
—what about HIM!   The glorious Lord Who can
make lame folks run, an' blind folks see, an' dead
folks live!   Talk about your temptations an' trials
if you like; but do 'e talk about Him too, Who is
able to keep us from fallin', holdin' us all the way
with His right hand.   Hills an' mountains!   Iss,
but what o' them when a man can wait 'pon the
Lord, an' go mountin' up with wings like a great
eagle, so that it don't make no difference whether

'tis up-hill or down-hill or 'pon level ground!
Hindrances an' difficulties! Iss; but what about
Him that maketh us more than conquerors! Do
let us count that we are 'pon the winnin' side, get
into the way o' thinkin' about the Mighty Jesus
an' keep there. Bless Him, He has brought ten
thousand thousand safe home, an' He can set you
an' me there, too—with white robes, an' crowns, an'
palms o' victory. If a man can go along brave an'
cheerful anywhere, let him go along brave an'
cheerful in the road to Heaven. Ah, what company.
' *All power is given unto Me, in Heaven and in Earth.*'
Listen to that, you young ones! What do 'ee think
of it? An' then think how it do finish—'*And lo:
I am with you alway, even unto the end of the
world.*' "

"My glorious Lord!" cried Mat adoringly,
unable to restrain himself any longer.

"*Then the third rule that I do want you to mind
is this*—ONE DAY TO A TIME. Seemin' to me that
our Heavenly Father have given us our life in days,
because He sees that we can't manage no more than
that to once. Lots o' people might get on very
well if they'd be content to take life like 'tis given;
but they go wonderin' whatever they shall do next
week, or whatever will happen to them next year, an'
so they get frightened, an' think that 'tis no good
their tryin', not a bit. I can mind once when I

A 2

was a little boy, helpin' mother to store away the
apples. I put my arms round ever so many o'
them an' tried to bring them all. I managed for
a step or two. Then out fell one an' another, and
two or three more, till they was all rollin' over the
floor. Mother laughed. 'Now, Dan'el,' says she,
'I'm goin' to teach you a lesson.' So she put my
little hands quite tight round one. 'There' said she,
'bring that, an' then fetch another.' I've often
thought about it when I've seen folks who might
be doin' ever so much good, if they didn't try to do
too much all to once. Don't go tryin' to put your
arms round a year; an' don't go troublin' about
next week. Wake up in the mornin' an' think
like this : *Here's another day come. Whatever I do
an' whatever I don't do, Lord, help me to do this—
help me to live it to Thee !*'

"Well, mind that—an' mind this too. Be sure
an' put this down. *Get a good start.* They that do
set up for to be weatherwise do tell what the day
will be by the sunrise. Like Jesus said to the
Pharisees—'Ye say, It will be foul weather to-
day : for the sky is red an' louring.' A good
start goes further than anything else for to make
a good day.

"Let the Sun o' Righteousness rise all fair an'
clear in the soul, an' 'tis easy to walk in the light
all day then. Here, young folks—I've seen bits o'

rhyme about the weather so as to help people to remember it better; an' here's a bit for you to think of every mornin'.

> 'Between six an' eight
> You have sealed its fate.'

Tell me how a man do get ready for the day, an' I'll tell you how he do get through it. Ah, there's poor Brother Mean-well—he'll read a chapter in the mornin', but he do never think about it. He'll kneel down to pray, and 'tis the same old set o' words 'zactly, day after day, an' year after year—all so pat an' so smooth, that there's no bite nor grip about 'em. 'Catch'd cold an' laid up!' why, is it any wonder when folks do let their souls go out in all the rain an' wind only half drest? 'Makin' very poor speed?' I should think so, when you can scarce stay for to fit a bit o' breakfast for the soul, an' then go starvin' it, poor thing, till supper time—an' then you're so tired that it might so well go without. 'The old enemy too much for 'ee!' O' course he is; goin' out where he is a-lyin' wait for 'ee, an' you don't take the trouble for to put up so much as a helmet or a breastplate! You don't carry so much as a shield or a spear! O' course you're knocked down afore the day is over. Serve 'ee right, too. Put that down, you young ones; put that down. *Get a good start.*

"*Set out with a good courage*—that's the next

2A 2

thing. I've heard them say that have been in the militia, that they wake 'em up every mornin' with the bugle call. That's the way, seemin' to me, that a Christian ought to wake up,—with music ringin' in his soul an' puttin' some courage in his veins. Poor Little-faith do wake up with a sigh an' a shiver. 'I am so different from most people,' says poor Little-faith—'an' here's another day come, an' there's so many cares an' so many hindrances!' Bless the Lord, I want you young folks to get into a way o' settin' out feelin' quite sure that His religion is made for *you*. An' not just for going to chapel in your Sunday clothes either ; but for work an' for worries ; for wants an' cares like yours an' mine. Little-faith does'nt give religion a chance. He's like them there folks that do go out in the water *ankle-deep*, and then wonder how 't is that they can't float an' swim like other people do. Plunge right into the sea o' His grace, young folks. Start the day thinkin' like this—'There'll be nothin' to-day, but He will help me. There'll be nowhere to-day, but He will be with me. No temptation, but He can deliver me. No burden, but I can cast it 'pon Him. Bless His name.' Let the music o' His precious promises ring in our souls and stir us up like the sound o' a trumpet.

" An' grace to help isn't all that I want us for to think about. Go out into the day, thinkin' how *the lovin' Father looks all along it, an' knows wha' we want.* I very often think about it—how when I was a little lad startin' off for school, mother used to go to the door an' look out. When 't was all bright sunshine, with the lark a-singin' up in the blue sky an' the bees hummin' all about the garden, she would just put on my cap an' give me a kiss an' send me skippin' over the fields. But 'pon the stormy days, when the wind came howlin', au' you could hear the ground-swell roarin', an' there was nothin' but great heavy clouds all over the sky, then she would tie the cap down round my ears, and button up my coat all so careful. Ah, I can see her now—how she used to stand watchin' me over the hills. Come, thou dear child o' God—that's just like 't is with our lovin' Father in Heaven. Bless Him, He do look out over the day. Whenever I think about it the words come to my heart : *Shall* HE *not much more clothe you, O ye of little faith?* Why, poor Little-faith, 't is put there on purpose for you. There's a worry waitin'. He do see it, an' here's the patience. There's a temptation on there. Yes, He do know that, an' here's wisdom and strength. There's a bit of a trial: an' here He is waitin' to give thee a bit o' courage and faith. An' don't let that be all. 'T is goin' to be a day o' sunshine an' gladness. Ah, He will make thee glad with His favour, an' send thee forth all cheerful to thy work. Bless Him."

Mest' Gribble was really quite as bad as Mat, for he turned and nodded to him over that. And though it was Mat who said, " Praise the Lord ! " it really was the farmer's beaming face and moistened eyes that set Mat off.

"Then mind this, young folks—*when you're gettin' ready for the day, get alone.* There aren't many forms an' ceremonies laid down in the Bible— leastways in the New Testament ; we may please ourselves about most o' them. But seemin' to me that there is one that the Lord Jesus have laid down so clear that we daren't do any other. 'T is in the sixth chapter o' Matthew. *When thou prayest, enter into thy closet, and when thou hast shut thy door, pray to thy Father in secret.* Get away with the Lord alone. We do want to shut our ears so well as our eyes. I can't pray when folks are a- comin' patterin' down the aisle, disturbin' everybody. 'T is best to stop, an' wait till they've got settled— then begin again. An' o' course you can't pray when there's talkin' an' bustlin' all around 'e. A man can lift up his heart to the Lord anywhere ; but if he do want to have a downright good bit o' prayer, he must get away alone with the Lord. Abraham rose up early in the mornin', when there was nobody else stirrin', I expect, an' he'd got it all quiet. Moses was to come up into the mount all by himself, nobody else was to be seen in all the

mountain, an' the very flocks an' herds weren't to
come near with their bleatin' an' bellowin'. Then
the Lord came down and made His goodness pass
before him. An' the Blessed Jesus Himself sent
the disciples away across the sea while He went
into a mountain apart to pray. Do 'e get alone
somewhere with the Lord. Out in the barn, like
dear old Mr. Carvosso used to; or in a sand-pit,
like I've read about Bramwell; or in a hole in
the ground, like I've heard tell o' dear old Dick
Hampton."

Then Dan'el's thoughts flew off at once to the
cave by the sea, where he had so often gained the
victory.

"Ah, bless the Lord, why, the place do come
to be so precious, an' there is so many glorious
memories hangin' about it, that the very thought
o' it is enough to set anybody a-prayin' straight off.
You do come to think o' so many blessin's and
deliverances that you've had 'pon that very spot,
you feel like as if you must prevail there. I can
understand that there about Daniel the prophet
gettin' right away to the old place over by the
window so soon as ever he knew that the writin'
was signed,—he felt in a minute that it was all
right in spite o' the presidents an' princes, an' all
the rest o' them. Young folks, *mind you do get
away alone with the Lord.*

Then the next rule is a very partic'lar one indeed. Be sure you do mind this—*Put the Word in the right place.* 'Tis all a failure without that. You might so well try for to keep a sprat alive upon the top o' Carn Brea, or to carry a lighted candle down to the bottom o' the sea, as to keep the grace o' God alive in your heart without feedin' 'pon the Word. Keep trimmin' the wick—that's needful; an' so 'tis to keep the light burnin', an' to keep the lamp clean; but *the Word is the oil,*—without that you'll very soon be in the dark. Get a bit o' the Word in your heart every day.

"I do often turn to the first Psalm. 'Tis like John Wesley's likeness in the beginnin' o' the Hymn-Book,—there in the beginnin' o' the Book o' Psalms, there's the likeness o' the Blessed man."

As Dan'el spoke, he turned over the pages of the Bible, and put on the big spectacles. "Look at it, you beginners, when you do get home to-night. If you do want to know how to keep out o' bad company you'll find it there. Away in the back part o' the picture, like in the distance, there's the ungodly talkin', and there's the sinners walkin', and there's the scorner,—he can't agree with any-body else, so do live single,—he is sittin'. But the *blessed man* have got his back 'pon them. *Meditation 'pon the Word* is the best cure for bad company. An' then on the other side o' the

picture there's a river, an' a tree planted. 'Tis
planted so firm an' so strong that it may blow
'great guns' as they say, but that tree won't stir.
Ah, if you want to be a steady-goin' Christian,
one o' the abidin' sort, there 'tis again, it must come
right out o' meditation 'pon the Word. Put the
Word in the right place an' you won't shift. An'
then you must look at the *leaves* o' that tree too.
No matter though the snow be on the ground, or
the east wind come nippin'—*His leaf shall not
wither.* There, if we do want to get our religion
right into all the little outermost things o' our life,
there's only one thing that'll do it—*meditate 'pon
the Word.* An' that isn't all, though 'tis a brave
deal, sure 'nough. Come winter so well as summer;
come spring so well as autumn, there's *fruit.* An'
fruit in his season—the right sort o' fruit. I do
know folks who do bear crops o' good advice for
hungry poor folks that want a loaf o' bread; an'
heaps o' golden plenty an' good dinners for them
that got enough o' their own. They'll put their
hands behind their back, an' lecture them that are
down; but they're hand-in-glove with the rich,
though they mayn't be so very religious. Fruit,
an' fruit in his season —that's what is wanted. A
crop o' blankets an' soup kitchens for winter. A
crop o' Patience for March winds; a bit o' Pity for
them that need it; an' Help an' Brotherliness an'

Love all the year round. That's the sort o' man
we do want. An' you'll find that sort o' man in
one place an' no other. 'Tis no good tryin', you
can't get him any other way. He do grow right
up out o' *meditation 'pon the Word o' the Lord.*
Stick to the Word, you young folks,—everything
else a'most will grow out o' that.

"*Then the next thing is about Prayin'.*—Mind
that too. There's a lot o' things goin' by the
name o' gold, but 'tis only in the looks. So there's
a good deal o' what people call prayer, but it
will only do for them that don't know the real
thing. I can only stay for a word or two about that
now.

"For years I used to fancy that 'twas proper to
begin to pray an' go right on without stoppin' till
I had done altogether. But one day I was down
to Redburn Market, an' so soon as I'd got one
thing that I wanted, I asked myself—'What next,
then?' an' 'what besides?' Then it come across
me in a minute. 'There, Dan'el,' I says to myself;
'*that's the way to pray.*' An' so 'tis; for since I've
done that, my prayers do seem to stick more, and are
more *real;* and it have brought me into a way o'
talkin' with the Lord about the day's work an'
things, that is uncommon helpful.

"I do like to begin with a bit o' praise, *delightin'
myself in the Lord,* as the Book do say. 'Tis always

easy to pray if we do get right away to Calvary;
leastways that will always wake up my dull heart.
To think o' what a glorious Lord He is, an' o' what
He have done. To think o' His Power an' His
love an' His Patience, an' to think how He do long
for to help me. Well, then, I do love to talk to
the Blessed Lord, an' to tell Him what I have got
to do, an' where I'm goin' to, an' to ask His advice.
Bless His name, we can take Him into partnership
'long with us. He will bring all the capital, an'
the best o' credit, too. I do believe, friends, that
the lovin' Lord Jesus do dearly like for us to
unlock all the doors o' the heart to Him. He is
such a *Brotherly* Saviour if we do only let Him
come like He wants to. I *do* find it so good for
to have Him sittin' down alongside o' me all the
day. Why, I wouldn't touch my awl again so long
as I live, if I couldn't feel that the Lord do care
how I do make a pair o' shoes, an' will help me to
make 'em so strong an' so good as ever I can. O,
do open all your hearts to Him, young folks;
iss, an' old folks too. Don't let there be any
secrets from Him. When you are kneelin' down
ask yourselves, ' What more do I want ? ' an'
' what besides is there ? '

An' do 'e be *real;* don't be afraid for to call
things by their right names. People do talk, an' do
pray, like as if religion was something up in the sky,

ever so far.   No, if 'tisn't down here, close alongside o' us, an' if it don't go out with a man to his
work—down the mine to the bottom level, or out to
the fields, or, into the workshop,—'tis wisht poor
trade, an' not worth the trouble o' keepin'. Religion
have got to do with everything—,with makin' butter
an' mindin' the babies so much as it have with
singin' hymns an' hearin' sermons. Do 'e be *real*
when you pray.

"Well, that's about gettin' ready. Now, I
want to give you young folks two rules for the day
itself, an' then one for to finish it with. This here
is from an old book that I'm very fond of, and a
capital rule it is too.* *Think of God when you hear
the clock strike.* Here is a bit o' rhyme that may
help you to mind it.

> ' Another hour doth begin,
>   Let it, O Lord, be free from sin.'

You see, our work an' the busy world is apt for to get
such a hold of us, as Cap'n Joe was sayin' the other
week, that 't is hard work to lose them. Well, let
the strikin' o' the clock help us a bit. Look up
when you do hear that. Take your bearin's a bit,
an' see if you're goin' all right. Take a fresh hold

---

* It was from Dan'el's well-worn copy of Jeremy Taylor's
Holy Living.

o' the Lord's help. Then at it again so hard as
you can.

"An' put this down too. *Get a dinner-time for
the soul.* Depen' 'pon it, friends—you can no more
go with nothin' but breakfast an' supper for your
soul, than for your body. You'll get all faint an'
lose your appetite an' be all upset without that.
There's lots o' these here poor, weak creatures that
can hardly manage for to crawl through the week
from Sunday to Sunday—why, they'd hold up their
heads an' be good-lookin' well-to-do people if they
would only try this. Get away with the Lord for a
quarter of an hour, get the dust o' the world washed
off, an' a bit o' waitin' 'pon the Lord, an' you'll
start again so fresh an' so strong. I came 'pon
the story the other day there in the fourth chapter
o' St. John; an' it seemed to set it all before me
'zackly. *At the sixth hour*—that's twelve o'clock,
we do get all parched with the heat. Then we
must bring our pitcher to the Well. Ah, we're
sure to find Jesus there, waitin' for us to ask of
Him, an' He will give us the livin' Water.

"Then the last rule is this, young folks—*End
the day with the judgment.* You do begin it by
lookin' forward. End it by lookin' back. Kneel
down an' ask the Lord all about it. What have
been right an' what have been wrong, an' what
might have been better. Tell the Lord where the

patience failed us; an' where the supply o' love ran short, an' where the courage was wantin'. Tell Him about the unwatchfulness; an' if there is sin, bring it right out. Call it by the proper name. Ask the Lord to make it *hurt*, so that you won't go doin' it again. Ah, bring it up there in sight o' the dreadful Cross, an' see that nothin' but the blood o' the glorious Redeemer can cleanse thee from it.

"But be sure o' this—*Don't go confessin' sins that you're not sorry for, an' that you haven't done.* 'Tisn't religious, though scores o' people think it is. 'Tisn't. There's only one name for that—*lies!* An' the worse kind o' lies too. Do 'e be real, young folks, an' speak from your hearts. There's lots o' people, who think if they do only kneel down an' call theirselves dreadful names, an' own to all sorts o' dreadful things, they're sure o' Heaven. An' all the time the Lord isn't listenin' to their words 't all, but He is lookin' right in 'pon their hearts! The Lord don't love people a bit more for tryin' to make theirselves out to be a great deal worse than other folks, specially if they do *think* that they're rather better. But there is one thing that He do love—He do love for us to be *sincere an' real,* an' for us to speak *right out of our hearts.*

"An' mind you do think o' something else beside the faults an' failins'. Look back an' see where you got the upper hand, an' be sure to praise the Lord for that. Tell the Lord all about that too, 'tis music to Him so well as for us—how Patience got the victory; an' Love didn't fail us anywhere; an' how Courage carried the day; an' Watchfulness kept a sharp look-out. Mind you bring that out too, an' praise the Lord for it all. Why, I do count 'tis a dreadful robbery, to come in the mornin' a-beggin' and prayin' for the help o' the Lord; an' then never to have a word in the evenin' about the victories that His help have won. I can't understand it I'm sure, but so 'tis. I really do believe that there's some people, an' sort o' religious people, too, who are more afraid o' thankin' God than they are o' sinnin' against Him—anyhow they're always tellin' the Lord o' their failin's, an' never speak a word o' their victories. They do think 'tis so nice an' humble. Iss, but there's one thing that's hundreds o' times better than that— *makin' our boast in the Lord.* He Who loveth us an' maketh us more than conquerors is worthy to receive blessin' an' honour, an' power an' glory. I do like the day to end with the judgment, because that is how life will end. But I do like the judgment to end in praise an' thanksgivin', because that's like heaven comin' after. So let the day end, friends, not in darkness and silence—that's like death an' the grave,—but in love an' praise to Him

that sitteth upon the throne an' to the Lamb.
That's like as if we was a day's march nearer to
the Father's House, where they have obtained joy
an' gladness, an' sorrow an' sighin' are fled away.'

HATMAN BROS. AND LILLY, HATTON HOUSE, FARRINGDON ROAD, E.C.

Standard & Popular Works

PUBLISHED BY

T. WOOLMER, 2, CASTLE STREET, CITY ROAD, E.C.

PRICE SIX SHILLINGS.

The Light of the World : Lessons from the Life of Our Lord
for Children. By the Rev. RICHARD NEWTON, D.D., Author of *Rays from
the Sun of Righteousness*, etc., etc., etc. Fcap. 4to. Numerous Illusts.
'A most attractive and deeply interesting Sunday book for children.'

PRICE FIVE SHILLINGS.

Consecrated Culture. Memorials of Benjamin Alfred Gregory,
M.A. By the Rev. Dr. GREGORY. Crown 8vo, with Portrait.

Gems Reset ; or, The Revised Wesleyan Catechisms Illustrated
by Imagery and Narrative. By Rev. B. SMITH. Crown 8vo.

Tales and Poems of South India. By Rev. E. J. ROBINSON.
Crown 8vo.

American Methodism, A Compendious History of. By
ABEL STEVENS, LL.D. Crown 8vo, with Portraits.

Sermons by the Rev. W. MORLEY PUNSHON, LL.D. With
a Preface by the Rev. W. ARTHUR, M.A. These Sermons contain the
latest Corrections of the Author. Two Volumes. Crown 8vo. 5/- each.
'Here we have found, in rare combination, pure and elevated diction,
conscience-searching appeal, withering exposure of sin, fearless advocacy of
duty, forceful putting of truth,' etc., etc.—*London Quarterly Review.*

Lectures by the Rev. W. MORLEY PUNSHON, LL.D.
Crown 8vo.
'One and all of the Lectures are couched in the powerful and popular style
which distinguished the great preacher, and they are worthy of a permanent
place in any library.'—*Daily Chronicle.*

Toward the Sunrise: being Sketches of Travel in Europe
and the East. To which is added a Memorial Sketch (with Portrait) of the
Rev. W. MORLEY PUNSHON, LL.D. By HUGH JOHNSTON, M.A., B.D.
Crown 8vo. Numerous Illustrations.

Fiji and the Fijians ; and Missionary Labours among the
Cannibals. Sixth Thousand. Revised and Supplemented with Index. By
Rev. JAMES CALVERT ; and a Preface by C. F. GORDON CUMMING, Author
of *At Home in Fiji*, etc. Crown 8vo, with Portrait of Thakombau, a Map,
and numerous Illustrations.

PRICE FOUR SHILLINGS.

Zoology of the Bible. By HARLAND COULTAS. Preface
by the Rev. W. F. MOULTON, D.D. Imperial 16mo. 126 Illustrations.

Missionary Anecdotes, Sketches, Facts, and Incidents.
By the Rev. WILLIAM MOISTER. Imperial 16mo. Eight Page Illustrations.
'The narratives are many of them very charming.'—*Sword and Trowel.*

The Brotherhood of Men ; or, Christian Sociology. By Rev
W. UNSWORTH.

3—86.

PRICE THREE SHILLINGS AND SIXPENCE.

Uncle Jonathan's Walks in and Around London. Foolscap 4to. Profusely Illustrated.

Our Indian Empire: its Rise and Growth. By the Rev. J. SHAW BANKS. Imperial 16mo. Thirty-five Illustrations and Map.
 'The imagination of the young will be fired by its stirring stories of English victories, and it will do much to make history popular.'—*Daily Chronicle.*

Northern Lights; or, Pen and Pencil Sketches of Twenty-one Modern Scottish Worthies. By Rev. J. MARRAT. Third Edition, enlarged. Crown 8vo. Portraits and Illustrations.
 'It is a charming book in every sense.'—*Irish Evangelist.*

Our Sea-Girt Isle: English Scenes and Scenery Delineated. By the Rev. J. MARRAT. Imperial 16mo. Map and 153 Illustrations.
 'An unusually readable and attractive book.'—*Christian World.*

Rambles in Bible Lands. By the Rev. RICHARD NEWTON, D.D. Imperial 16mo. Seventy Illustrations.
 'From the juvenile stand-point, we can speak in hearty commendation of it.'—*Literary World.*

'Land of the Mountain and the Flood': Scottish Scenes and Scenery Delineated. By the Rev. JABEZ MARRAT. Imperial 16mo. Map and Seventy-six Illustrations.
 'Described with taste, judgment, and accuracy of detail.'—*Scotsman.*

Popery and Patronage. Biographical Illustrations of Scotch Church History. By the Rev. J. MARRAT. Imperial 16mo. Ten Illustrations.
 'Most instructive biographical narratives.'—*Derbyshire Courier.*

Wycliffe to Wesley: Heroes and Martyrs of the Church in Britain. Imperial 16mo. Twenty-four Portraits and Forty other Illustrations.
 'We give a hearty welcome to this handsomely got up and interesting volume.'—*Literary World.*

John Lyon; or, From the Depths. By RUTH ELLIOTT. Sixth Thousand. Crown 8vo. Five Full-page Illustrations.
 'Earnest and eloquent, dramatic in treatment, and thoroughly healthy in spirit.'—*Birmingham Daily Gazette.*

The Thorough Business Man: Memoir of Walter Powell, Merchant. By Rev. B. GREGORY. Eighth Edition. Crn. 8vo, with Portrait.

The Life of Gideon Ouseley. By the Rev. WILLIAM ARTHUR, M.A. Ninth Thousand. Crown 8vo, with Portrait.

The Aggressive Character of Christianity. By Rev. W. UNSWORTH.

Simon Holmes, the Carpenter of Aspendale. By J. JACKSON WRAY. Crown 8vo.

Garton Rowley; or, Leaves from the Log of a Master Mariner. By J. JACKSON WRAY. Crown 8vo.

Honest John Stallibrass. By J. JACKSON WRAY. Crown 8vo.

A Man Every Inch of Him. By J. JACKSON WRAY. Crn. 8vo.

Paul Meggitt's Delusion. By J. JACKSON WRAY. Crown 8vo.

Nestleton Magna. A Story of Yorkshire Methodism. By J. JACKSON WRAY. Crown 8vo.

Chronicles of Capstan Cabin; or, the Children's Hour. By J. JACKSON WRAY. Imperial 16mo. Twenty-eight Illustrations.

PRICE THREE SHILLINGS AND SIXPENCE (*Continued*.)

Scenes and Adventures in Great Namaqualand. By the Rev. B. RIDSDALE. Crown 8vo, with Portrait.

Missionary Stories, Narratives, Scenes, and Incidents. By the Rev. W. MOISTER. Crown 8vo. Eight Page Illustrations.

Melissa's Victory. By ASHTON NEILL. Crown 8vo, gilt edges. Illustrations by GUNSTON.

Two Saxon Maidens. By ELIZA KERR. Crown 8vo, gilt edges. Illustrations by GUNSTON.

Vice-Royalty; or, a Royal Domain held for the King, and enriched by the King. Crown 8vo. Twelve page Illustns. By Rev. B. SMITH.

Sunshine in the Kitchen; or, Chapters for Maid Servants. Fourth Thousand. Crown 8vo. Numerous Illustrations. By Rev. B. SMITH.

Way-Marks : Placed by Royal Authority on the King's Highway. Being One Hundred Scripture Proverbs, Enforced and Illustrated. Crown 8vo. Eight Page Engravings. By Rev. B. SMITH.

The Great Army of London Poor. Sketches of Life and Character in a Thames-side District. By the River-side Visitor. Third Edition. Crown 8vo. 540 pp. Eight Illustrations.

PRICE TWO SHILLINGS AND SIXPENCE.

The Man with the White Hat; or, The Story of an Unknown Mission. By C. R. PARSONS. Crown 8vo. 21 Illustrations. Gilt edges.

The Opposite House ; and other Stories for Cottage Homes. By A. FRANCES PERRAM.

Fifty Years of Mission-Life in South Africa. By the Rev. JOHN EDWARDS. Second Edition, with Portrait. Crown 8vo.

The Hallam Succession. A Story of Methodist Life in Two Countries. By A. E. BARR. Crown 8vo. Frontispiece.

Fought and Won. A Story of School Life. By RUTH ELLIOTT. Crown 8vo, with Frontispiece.

'Than Many Sparrows.' By ANNIE E. COURTENAY, Author of 'Tina and Beth.' Crown 8vo, with Frontispiece.

Elias Power, of Ease-in-Zion. By Rev. JOHN M. BAMFORD. Eighth Thousand. Crown 8vo. Seventeen Illustrations. Gilt edges.

John Conscience, of Kingseal. By Rev. JOHN M. BAMFORD, Author of ' Elias Power.' Crown 8vo. Seventeen Illustrations, gilt edges.

Rambles and Scrambles in the Tyrol. By Mrs. HENRY HILL. Crown 8vo, numerous Illustrations.

Good News for Children; or, God's Love to the Little Ones. By JOHN COLWELL. Crown 8vo, gilt edges. Fourteen Illustrations.

Pleasant Talks about Jesus. By JOHN COLWELL. Crown 8vo.

Life of John Wicklif. By Rev. W. L. WATKINSON. Portrait and Eleven Illustrations. Crown 8vo.

Little Abe ; or, the Bishop of Berry Brow. Being the Life of Abraham Lockwood, a quaint and popular Local Preacher. By F. JEWELL. Crown 8vo, gilt edges. With Portrait.

Cecily : a Tale of the English Reformation. By EMMA LESLIE. Crown 8vo. Five full-page Illustrations.

Glimpses of India and Mission Life. By Mrs. HUTCHEON. Crown 8vo. Eight Page Illustrations.

The Secret of the Mere ; or, **Under** the Surface. By J. JACKSON WRAY.

PRICE TWO SHILLINGS AND SIXPENCE (*Continued.*)

The Beloved Prince: a Memoir of His Royal Highness, the Prince Consort. By WILLIAM NICHOLS. Crown 8vo. With Portrait and Nineteen Illustrations. Cloth, gilt edges.

Glenwood: a Story of School Life. **By** JULIA K. BLOOM-FIELD. Crown 8vo. Seven Illustrations.

'A useful book for school-girls who think more of beauty and dress than of brains and grace.'—*Sword and Trowel.*

Undeceived: Roman or Anglican? A Story of English Ritualism. By RUTH ELLIOTT. Sixth Thousand. Crown 8vo.

'In the creation and description of character the work belongs to the highest class of imaginative art.'—*Free Church of England Magazine.*

Self-Culture and Self-Reliance, under God the Means of Self-Elevation. By the Rev. W. UNSWORTH. Crown 8vo.

'An earnest, thoughtful, eloquent book on an important subject.'—*Folkestone News.*

A Pledge that Redeemed Itself. By SARSON, Author of 'Blind Olive', etc. Crown 8vo. Numerous Illustrations. Gilt edges.

Old Daniel; or, Memoirs of a Converted Hindu. By the Rev. T. HODSON. Crown 8vo, gilt edges. Coloured Illustrations.

The Story of a Peninsular Veteran: Sergeant in the 43rd Light Infantry during the Peninsular War. Crown 8vo. 13 Illustrations.

'Full of adventure, told in a religious spirit. We recommend this narrative to boys and young men.'—*Hastings and St. Leonard's News.*

Rays from the Sun of Righteousness. By the Rev. RICHARD NEWTON, D.D. Crown 8vo. Eleven Illustrations. Gilt edges.

In the Tropics; or, Scenes and Incidents of West Indian Life. By the Rev. JABEZ MARRAT. Crown 8vo, gilt edges, Illustrations, etc.

Climbing: a Manual for the Young who Desire to Rise in Both Worlds. By the Rev. BENJAMIN SMITH. Crown 8vo. Sixth Edition.

Our Visit to Rome, with Notes by the Way. By the Rev. JOHN RHODES. Royal 16mo. Forty-five Illustrations.

The Lancasters and their Friends. A Tale of Methodist Life. By S. J. F. Third Thousand. Crown 8vo.

Those Boys. By FAYE HUNTINGTON. Crown 8vo. Illustrated.

Leaves from my Log of Twenty-five years' Christian Work in the Port of London. Seventh Thousand. Crown 8vo. Eight Illustrations.

East End Pictures; or, More Leaves from My Log of Twenty-five Years' Christian Work. By T. C. GARLAND. Third Thousand. Crown 8vo. Portrait and Five Illustrations.

The Willow Pattern: A Story Illustrative of Chinese Social Life. By the Rev. HILDERIC FRIEND. Crown 8vo, gilt edges. Numerous Illustrations.

Passages from the Diary of an Early Methodist. By RICHARD ROWE.

Orphans of the Forest; or, His Little Jonathan. By A. E. COURTENAY. Foolscap 8vo. Four Illustrations.

MARK GUY PEARSE'S WORKS.
Ten Volumes, Crown 8vo, Cloth, Gilt Edges. Price 2s. 6d. each.

1.—Daniel Quorm, and his Religious Notions. FIRST SERIES. 71,000.

2.—Daniel Quorm, and his Religious Notions. SECOND SERIES. 26,000.

3.—Sermons for Children. 20,000.

4.—Mister Horn and his Friends; or, Givers and Giving. 21,000.

5.—Short Stories, and other Papers. 8000.

6.—'Good Will': a Collection of Christmas Stories. 10,000.

7.—Simon Jasper. 11,000.

8.—Cornish Stories. 6000.

9.—Homely Talks. 10,000.

10.—John Tregenoweth, Rob Rat, and The Old Miller and his Mill.

'Scarcely any living writer can construct a parable better, more quaintly, simply, and congruously. His stories are equally clever and telling. . . . One secret of their spell is that they are brimful of heart. . . . His books should be in every school library.'—*British Quarterly Review.*

Thoughts on Holiness. By MARK GUY PEARSE. Fifteenth Thousand. Royal 16mo. Cloth, red edges.

Some Aspects of the Blessed Life. By MARK GUY PEARSE. Royal 16mo. Cloth, red edges.

PRICE TWO SHILLINGS.

Wayside Wisdom; or, Old Solomon's Ideas of Things. By Rev. JOHN COLWELL. Crown 8vo. Numerous Illustrations.

Punchi Nona: A Story of Female Education and Village Life in Ceylon. By Rev. S. LANGDON. Crown 8vo. Numerous Illustns.

Friends and Neighbours: A Story for Young Children. Crown 8vo. Illustrated.

Andrew Golding: A Story of the Great Plague. By ANNIE E. KEELING. Crown 8vo. Three Illustrations.

The Pride of the Family. By ANNIE E. KEELING. Crown 8vo. Five Illustrations.

The Oakhurst Chronicles: A Tale of the Times of Wesley. By ANNIE E. KEELING. Crown 8vo. Four Illustrations.

Poet Toilers in Many Fields. By Mrs. R. A. WATSON. Crown 8vo. Thirteen Illustrations.

The 'Good Luck' of the Maitlands: a Family Chronicle. By Mrs. R. A. WATSON. Five Illustrations. Crown 8vo.

Valeria, the Martyr of the Catacombs. A Tale of Early Christian Life in Rome. By Dr. WITHROW. Crown 8vo. Illustrations.

Tina and Beth; or, the Night Pilgrims. By ANNIE E. COURTENAY. Crown 8vo. Frontispiece.

Wilfred Hedley; or, How Teetotalism Came to Ellensmere. By S. J. FITZGERALD. Crown 8vo. Frontispiece.

Equally Yoked: and other Stories. By S. J. FITZGERALD. Frontispiece.

Master and Man. By S. J. FITZGERALD. Frontispiece.

Coals and Colliers; or, How we Get the Fuel for our Fires. By S. J. FITZGERALD. Crown 8vo. Illustrations.

PRICE **TWO** SHILLINGS *(Continued)*.

James Daryll; or, From Honest Doubt to Christian Faith.
By RUTH ELLIOTT. Crown 8vo.
'We have seldom read a more beautiful story than this.'—*The Echo*.

The King's Messenger: a Story of Canadian Life. By the
Rev. W. H. WITHROW, M.A. Crown 8vo.

Illustrations of Fulfilled Prophecy. By the **Rev. J. ROBINSON**
GREGORY. Crown 8vo. Numerous Illustrations.

The Basket of Flowers. Illustrated. Crown 8vo, gilt **edges.**

The Great Apostle; or, Pictures from the Life of St. Paul.
By the Rev. JABEZ MARRAT. Foolscap 8vo. 28 Illustrations and Map.
'A charming little book. . . . Written in a style that must commend itself
to young people.'—*Sunday-School Times*.

Sir Walter Raleigh: Pioneer of Anglo-American Colonisation.
By CHARLES K. TRUE, D.D. Foolscap 8vo. 16 Illustrations.

Homes and Home Life in Bible Lands. By J. R. S.
CLIFFORD. Foolscap 8vo. Eighty Illustrations.
'A useful little volume respecting the manners and customs of Eastern
nations. It brings together, in a small compass, much that will be of service
to the young student of the Bible.'—*Watchman*.

Hid Treasures, and the Search for Them: Lectures to
Bible Classes. By the Rev. J. HARTLEY. Foolscap 8vo. With Frontispiece.

Youthful Obligations. Illustrated by a large number of **Appro-**
priate Facts and Anecdotes. Foolscap 8vo. With Illustrations.

Eminent Christian Philanthropists: Brief Biographical
Sketches, designed especially as Studies for the Young. By the Rev.
GEORGE MAUNDER. Fcap. 8vo. Nine Illustrations.

The Tower, the Temple, and the Minster: Historical and
Biographical Associations of the Tower of London, St. Paul's Cathedral,
and Westminster Abbey. By the Rev. J. W. THOMAS. Second Edition.
Foolscap 8vo. 14 Illustrations.

Peter Pengelly; or, 'True as the Clock.' By J. J. WRAY.
Crown 8vo. Forty Illustrations.
'A famous book for boys.'—*The Christian*.

The Stolen Children. By Rev. H. BLEBY. Foolscap 8vo.
Six Illustrations.

My Coloured Schoolmaster: and other Stories. By the Rev.
H. BLEBY. Foolscap 8vo. Five Illustrations.
'The narratives are given in a lively, pleasant manner that is well suited to
gain and keep alive the attention of juvenile readers.'—*The Friend*.

Female Heroism and Tales of the Western World. By
the Rev. H. BLEBY. Foolscap 8vo. Four Illustrations.

Capture of the Pirates: with other Stories of the Western Seas.
By the Rev. HENRY BLEBY. Foolscap 8vo. Four Illustrations.
'The stories are graphically told, and will inform on some phases of
Western life.'—*Warrington Guardian*.

The Prisoner's Friend: The Life of Mr. JAMES BUNDY, of
Bristol. By his Grandson, the Rev. W. R. WILLIAMS. Foolscap 8vo.

Adelaide's Treasure, and How the Thief came Unawares.
By SARSON, Author of 'A Pledge that Redeemed Itself', etc. Four Illustrations.

PRICE TWO SHILLINGS (*Continued.*)

Kilkee. By ELIZA KERR.

Two Snowy Christmas Eves. By ELIZA KERR. Royal 16mo. Gilt edges. Six Illustrations.

The Secret of Ashton Manor House. By ELIZA KERR. Crown 8vo.

The Mystery of Grange Drayton. By ELIZA KERR. Crown 8vo.

Ivy Chimneys. By EDITH CORNFORTH.

PRICE EIGHTEENPENCE.

'*Little Ray*' *Series. Royal 16mo.*

Little Ray and her Friends. By RUTH ELLIOTT. Five Illustrations.

The Breakfast Half-Hour: Addresses on Religious and Moral Topics. By the Rev. H. R. BURTON. Twenty-five Illustrations.
  '*Practical, earnest, and forcible.*'—*Literary World.*

Gleanings in Natural History for Young People. Profusely Illustrated.

Broken Purposes; or, the Good Time Coming. By LILLIE MONTFORT. Five Page Illustrations. Gilt edges.

The History of the Tea-Cup: with a Descriptive Account of the Potter's Art. By the Rev. G. R. WEDGWOOD. Profusely Illustrated.

The Cliftons and their Play-Hours. By Mrs. COSSLETT, Seven Page Illustrations.

The Lilyvale Club and its Doings. By EDWIN A. JOHNSON, D.D. Seven Page Illustrations.
  'The "doings" of the club decidedly deserve a careful perusal.'—*Literary World.*

The Bears' Den. By E. H. MILLER. Six Page Illustrations.
  'A capital story for boys.'—*Christian Age.*

Ned's Motto; or, Little by Little. By the author of 'Faithful and True,' 'Tony Starr's Legacy.' Six Page Illustrations.
  'The story of a boy's struggles to do right, and his influence over other boys. The book is well and forcibly written.'—*The Christian.*

A Year at Riverside Farm. By E. H. MILLER. Royal 16mo. Six Page Illustrations.
  'A book of more than common interest and power.'—*Christian Age.*

The Royal Road to Riches. By E. H. MILLER. Fifteen Illustrations.

Maude Linden; or, Working for Jesus. By LILLIE MONTFORT. Four Illustrations.
  'Intended to enforce the value of personal religion, especially in Christian work. . . . Brightly and thoughtfully written.'—*Liverpool Daily Post.*

Oscar's Boyhood; or, the Sailor's Son. By DANIEL WISE, D.D. Six Illustrations.
  'A healthy story for boys, written in a fresh and vigorous style, and plainly teaching many important lessons.'—*Christian Miscellany.*

PRICE EIGHTEENPENCE *(Continued)*.

Summer Days at Kirkwood. By E. H. MILLER. Four Illustrations.
> 'Capital story ; conveying lessons of the highest moral import.'—*Sheffield Post*.

Holy-days and Holidays; or, Memories of the Calendar for Young People. By J. R. S. CLIFFORD. Numerous Illustrations.
> 'Instruction and amusement are blended in this little volume.'—*The Christian*.

Talks with the Bairns about Bairns. By RUTH ELLIOTT. Illustrated.
> 'Pleasantly written, bright, and in all respects attractive.'—*Leeds Mercury*.

My First Class : and other Stories. By RUTH ELLIOTT. Illustrated.
> 'The stories are full of interest, well printed, nicely illustrated, and tastefully bound. It is a volume which will be a favourite in any family of children.'—*Derbyshire Courier*.

Luther Miller's Ambition. By LILLIE MONTFORT. Gilt edges. Illustrated by GUNSTON.

' Wee Donald' Series.' Royal 16mo.

An Old Sailor's Yarn : and other Sketches from Daily Life.

The Stony Road : a Tale of Humble Life.

Stories for Willing Ears. For Boys. By T. S. E.

Stories for Willing Ears. For Girls. By T. S. E.

Thirty Thousand Pounds : and other Sketches from Daily Life.

' Wee Donald ' : Sequel to ' Stony Road.'

PRICE EIGHTEENPENCE. *Foolscap 8vo Series.*

Martin Luther, the Prophet of Germany. By the Rev. J. SHAW BANKS. Foolscap 8vo. 13 Illustrations.
> 'Told in a very attractive style.'—*London Quarterly Review*.

Two Standard Bearers in the East : Sketches of Dr. DUFF and Dr. WILSON. By Rev. J. MARRAT. Eight Illustrations.

Three Indian Heroes: the Missionary; the Soldier; the Statesman. By the Rev. J. SHAW BANKS. Numerous Illustrations.

David Livingstone, Missionary and Discoverer. By the Rev. J. MARRAT. Fifteen Page Illustrations.
> 'The story is told in a way which is likely to interest young people, and to quicken their sympathy with missionary work.'—*Literary World*.

Columbus; or, the Discovery of America. By GEORGE CUBITT. Seventeen Illustrations.

Cortes; or, the Discovery and Conquest of Mexico. By GEORGE CUBITT. Nine Illustrations.

Pizarro; or, the Discovery and Conquest of Peru. By GEORGE CUBITT. Nine Illustrations.

Granada; or, the Expulsion of the Moors from Spain. By GEORGE CUBITT. Seven Illustrations.

James Montgomery, Christian Poet and Philanthropist. By the Rev. J. MARRAT. Eleven Illustrations.

PRICE EIGHTEENPENCE (*Continued.*)

The Father of Methodism : the Life and Labours of the Rev. John Wesley, A.M. By Mrs. COSSLETT. Forty-five Illustrations.
  'Presents a clear outline of the life of the founder of Methodism. The illustrations are numerous and effective,—quite a pictorial history in themselves.'

Old Truths in New Lights : Illustrations of Scripture Truth for the Young. By W. H. S. Illustrated.

Chequer Alley : a Story of Successful Christian Work. By the Rev. F. W. BRIGGS, M.A.

The Englishman's Bible : How he Got it, and Why he Keeps it. By the Rev. JOHN BOVES, M.A. Thirteen Illustrations.

Home : and the Way to Make Home Happy. By the Rev. DAVID HAY. With Frontispiece.

Helen Leslie, or, Truth and Error. By ADELINE. Frontispiece.

Building her House. By Mrs. R. A. WATSON. Five Illustns.
  'A charmingly written tale, illustrative of the power of Christian meekness.'
  —*Christian World.*

Crabtree Fold : a Tale of the Lancashire Moors. By Mrs. R. A. WATSON. Five Illustrations.

Davy's Friend : and other Stories. By JENNIE PERRETT.
  'Excellent, attractive, and instructive.'—*The Christian.*

Arthur Hunter's First Shilling. By Mrs. CROWE.

Hill Side Farm. By ANNA J. BUCKLAND.

The Boy who Wondered ; or, Jack and Minnchen. By Mrs. GEORGE GLADSTONE.

Kitty ; or, The Wonderful Love. By A. E. COURTENAY.

The River Singers. By W. ROBSON.

PRICE EIGHTEENPENCE. *Crown 8vo Series.*

'Twixt Promise and Vow ; and other Stories. By RUTH ELLIOTT.

Eleanor's Ambition. By SARSON C. J. INGHAM. With Frontispiece. Cloth gilt.

Siam and the Siamese as described by American Missionaries. With Map and Illustrations.

Life in a Parsonage ; or, Lights and Shadows of the Itinerancy. By Dr. WITHROW.

May's Captain. By HELEN BRISTON. Three Illustrations.

The Little World of School. By R. RYLANDS. Three Illustrations.

Patty Thorne's Adventures. By Mrs. H. B. PAULL. Illustrated.

The Dairyman's Daughter. By the Rev. LEGH RICHMOND, M.A. A New Edition, with Additions, giving an Authentic Account of her Conversion, and of her connection with the Wesleyan Methodists.

Footsteps in the Snow. By ANNIE E. COURTENAY, Author of *Tina and Beth*, etc., etc. Illustrated.
  'Every page is genial, warm, and bright.'—*Irish Christian Advocate.*

The Beloved Prince : A Memoir of His Royal Highness the Prince Consort. By WILLIAM NICHOLS. Nineteen Illustrations.

Drierstock : A Tale of Mission Work on the American Frontier. Three Illustrations.

The New Head Master ; or, Little Speedwell's Victory. By MARGARET HAYCRAFT.

PRICE EIGHTEENPENCE (*Continued.*)

Go Work: A Book for Girls. By ANNIE FRANCES PERRAM.

Picture Truths. Practical Lessons on the Formation of Character, from Bible Emblems and Proverbs. By JOHN TAYLOR. Thirty Illustrations.

Those Watchful Eyes; or, Jemmy and his Friends. By EMILIE SEARCHFIELD. Frontispiece.

The Basket of Flowers. Four Illustrations.

Auriel, and other Stories. By RUTH ELLIOTT. Frontispiece.

A Voice from the Sea; or, The Wreck of the Eglantine. By RUTH ELLIOTT.

Rays from the Sun of Righteousness. By the Rev. R. NEWTON. Eleven Illustrations.

A Pledge that Redeemed Itself. By SARSON.

In the Tropics; or, Scenes and Incidents of West Indian Life. By the Rev. J. MARRAT. Illustrations and Map.

Old Daniel; or, Memoirs of a Converted Hindu. By Rev. T. HODSON. Twelve Illustrations.

Little Abe; or, The Bishop of Berry Brow. Being the Life of Abraham Lockwood.

CHEAP EDITION OF MARK GUY PEARSE'S EOOKS.
Foolscap 8vo. Price Eighteenpence each.

1. **Daniel Quorm, and his Religious Notions.** 1ST SERIES.
2. **Daniel Quorm, and his Religious Notions.** 2ND SERIES.
3. **Sermons for Children.**
4. **Mister Horn and his Friends;** or, Givers and Giving.
5. **Short Stories:** and other Papers.
6. **'Good Will':** a Collection of Christmas Stories.
7. **Simon Jasper.**
8. **Cornish Stories.**
9. **Homely Talks.**
10. **John Tregenoweth, Rob Rat, and The Old Miller and his Mill.**

PRICE ONE SHILLING. *Imperial 32mo. Cloth, gilt lettered.*

Abbott's Histories for the Young.
Vol. 1. Alexander the Great. Vol. 2. Alfred the Great. Vol. 3. Julius Cæsar.

PRICE ONE SHILLING. *Royal 16mo. Cloth, gilt lettered.*

Ancient Egypt: Its Monuments, Worship, and People. By the Rev. EDWARD LIGHTWOOD. Twenty-six Illustrations.

Vignettes from English History. From the Norman Conqueror to Henry IV. Twenty-three Illustrations.

Margery's Christmas Box. By RUTH ELLIOTT. Seven Illusts.

No Gains without Pains: a True Life for the Boys. By H. C. KNIGHT. Six Illustrations.

Peeps into the Far North: Chapters on Iceland, Lapland, and Greenland. By S. E. SCHOLES. Twenty-four Illustrations.

Lessons from Noble Lives, and other Stories. 31 Illustrations.

PRICE ONE SHILLING (*Continued.*)

Stories of **Love** and Duty. For Boys and Girls. 31 Illusts.

The Railway Pioneers; or, the Story of the Stephensons, Father and Son. By H.C. KNIGHT. Fifteen Illustrations.

The Royal Disciple: Louisa, Queen of Prussia. ByC.R.HURST. Six Illustrations.

Tiny Tim: a Story of London Life. Founded on Fact. By F. HORNER. Twenty-two Illustrations.

John Tregenoweth. His Mark. By MARK GUY PEARSE. Twenty-five Illustrations.

'I 'll Try '; or, How the Farmer's Son became a Captain. Ten Illustrations.

The Giants, and How to Fight Them. By Dr. RICHARD NEWTON. Fifteen Illustrations.

The Meadow Daisy. By LILLIE MONTFORT. Numerous Illustrations.

Robert Dawson; or, the **Brave Spirit**. Four Page Illustrations.

The Tarnside Evangel. By M. A. H. Eight Illustrations.

Rob Rat: a Story of Barge Life. By MARK GUY PEARSE. Numerous Illustrations.

The Unwelcome Baby, with other Stories of Noble Lives early Consecrated. By S. ELLEN GREGORY. Nine Illustrations.

Jane Hudson, **the** American Girl. Four Page Illustrations.

The Babes in **the Basket ;** or, Daph and her Charge. Four Page Illustrations.

Insect Lights and Sounds. By J. R. S. CLIFFORD. Illustrns. 'A valuable little book for children, pleasantly illustrated.'—*The Friend.*

The Jew and his Tenants. By A. D. WALKER. Illustrated. 'A pleasant little story of the results of genuine Christian influence.'— *Christian Age.*

The History of Joseph: for the Young. By the Rev. T. CHAMPNESS. Twelve Illustrations. 'Good, interesting, and profitable.'—*Wesleyan Methodist Magazine.*

The Old Miller and his Mill. By MARK GUY PEARSE. Twelve Illustrations.

The First Year of my **Life:** a True Story for Young People. By ROSE CATHAY FRIEND.

Fiji and the Friendly Isles: Sketches of their Scenery and People. By S. E. SCHOLES. Fifteen Illustrations.

The Story of a Pillow. Told for Children. Four Illustrations. 'Simply and gracefully told.'—*Bradford Observer.*

The Archer's Chance Shot. By SARSON C. J. INGHAM. With Frontispiece.

Waiting, an Allegorical **Story.** By SARSON C. J. INGHAM. Four illustrations. Gilt edges.

UNCLE DICK'S LIBRARY OF SHILLING BOOKS.

Foolscap 8vo, 128 pp. Cloth.

Uncle Dick's Legacy. By E. H. MILLER, Author of 'Royal Road to Riches,' etc., etc. Illustrated.
'A first-rate story . . . full of fun and adventure, but thoroughly good and healthy.'—*Christian Miscellany.*

Beatrice and Brian. By HELEN BRISTON. Three Illustrns.
'A very prettily told story about a wayward little lady and a large mastiff dog, specially adapted for girls.'—*Derbyshire Advertiser.*

Becky and Reubie; or, the Little Street Singers. By MINA E. GOULDING. Three Illustrations.
'A clever, pleasing, well-written story.'—*Leeds Mercury.*

Gilbert Guestling; or, the Story of a Hymn Book. Illustrated.

Guy Sylvester's Golden Year. Three Illustrations.

Left to Take Care of Themselves. By A. RYLANDS. Three Illustrations.

Tom Fletcher's Fortunes. By Mrs. H. B. PAULL. Three Illustrations.
'A capital book for boys.'—*Sheffield and Rotherham Independent.*

The Young Bankrupt, and other Stories. By Rev. JOHN COLWELL. Three Illustrations.

The Basket of Flowers. Four Illustrations.

Mattie and Bessie. By A. E. COURTENAY.

Tom: A Woman's Work for Christ. By Rev. J. W. KEYWORTH. Six Illustrations.

The Little Disciple: The Story of his Life Told for Young Children. Six Illustrations.

Won Over. By Miss HELLIS. Foolscap 8vo, Three Page Illustrations.

Afterwards. By EMILIE SEARCHFIELD. Three Page Illustns.

Poppie's Life Service. By EMILIE SEARCHFIELD. Ten Illustrations.

PRICE ONE SHILLING.

Thoughts on Holiness. By MARK GUY PEARSE.

Mischievous Foxes; or, the Little Sins that mar the Christian Character. By JOHN COLWELL.
'An amazing amount of sensible talk and sound advice.'—*The Christian.*

Joel Bulu: The Autobiography of a Native Minister in the South Seas. New Edition, with an account of his Last Days. Edited by the Rev. G. S. ROWE. Foolscap 8vo, cloth.

Robert Moffat, the African Missionary. By Rev. J. MARRAT. Foolscap 8vo, Illustrated.

The Dairyman's Daughter. By the Rev. LEGH RICHMOND, M.A. A New Edition, with Additions, giving an Authentic Account of her Conversion, and of her connection with the Wesleyan Methodists.

Polished Stones from a Rough Quarry. By Mrs. HUTCHEON.

Recollections of Methodist Worthies. Fcap 8vo. 'Deserves to be perused by members of all Christian communities.'—*Sword and Trowel.*

A Bible Woman's Story: Autobiography of Mrs. COLLIER, of Birmingham.

Sketches of Early Methodism in the Black Country, and the Story of Leek-Seed Chapel.

PRICE NINEPENCE. *Imperial 32mo. Cloth, gilt lettered.*

1. The Wonderful Lamp: and other Stories. By RUTH ELLIOTT. Five Illustrations.
2. Dick's Troubles: and How He Met Them. By RUTH ELLIOTT. Six Illustrations.
3. The Chat in the Meadow: and other Stories. By LILLIE MONTFORT. Six Illustrations.
4. John's Teachers: and other Stories. By LILLIE MONTFORT. Six Illustrations.
5. Nora Grayson's Dream: and other Stories. By LILLIE MONTFORT. Seven Illustrations.
6. Rosa's Christmas Invitations: and other Stories. By LILLIE MONTFORT. Six Illustrations.
7. Ragged Jim's Last Song: and other Ballads. By EDWARD BAILEY. Eight Illustrations.
8. Pictures from Memory. By ADELINE. Nine Illustrations.
9. The Story of the Wreck of the 'Maria' Mail Boat: with a Memoir of Mrs. Hincksman, the only Survivor. Illustrated.
10. Passages from the Life of Heinrich Stilling. Five Page Illustrations.
11. Little and Wise: The Ants, The Conies, The Locusts, and the Spiders. Twelve Illustrations.
12. Spoiling the Vines, and Fortune Telling. Eight Illusts.
13. The Kingly Breaker, Concerning Play, and Sowing the Seed.
14. The Fatherly Guide, Rhoda, and Fire in the Soul.
15. Short Sermons for Little People. By the Rev. T. CHAMPNESS.
16. Sketches from my Schoolroom. Four Illustrations.
17. Mary Ashton: A True Story of Eighty Years Ago. 4 Illusts.
18. The Little Prisoner: or, the Story of the Dauphin of France. Five Illustrations.
19. The Story of an Apprenticeship. Frontispiece
20. Mona Bell: or, Faithful in Little Things. By EDITH M. EDWARDS. Four Illustrations.
21. Minnie Neilson's Summer Holidays, and What Came of Them. By M. CAMBWELL. Four Illustrations.
22. After Many Days; or, The Turning Point in James Power's Life. Three Illustrations.
23. Alfred May. By R. RYLANDS. Two coloured Illustrations.
24. Dots and Gwinnie: a Story of Two Friendships. By R. RYLANDS. Three Illustrations.
25. Little Sally. By MINA E. GOULDING. Six Illustrations.
26. Joe Webster's Mistake. By EMILIE SEARCHFIELD. Three Illustrations.
27. Muriel; or, The Sister Mother. Three Illustrations.
28. Nature's Whispers. Five Illustrations.
29. Johnny's Work and How he did it. Five Illustrations.
30. Pages from a Little Girl's Life. By A. F. PERRAM. Five Illustrations.
31. The Wrens' Nest at Wrenthorpe. By A. E. KEELING. Five Illustrations.
32. Bernard the Little Guide and other Stories. Four Illustrations.

PRICE EIGHTPENCE. *Imperial 32mo. Cloth, gilt edges.*

The whole of the Ninepenny Series are also sold in Limp Cloth at Eightpence.

Ancass, the **Slave** Preacher. By the Rev. HENRY BUNTING.

Archie and Nellie ; What they Saw and What they Heard. By RUTH ELLIOTT.

Bernard Palissy, the Huguenot Potter. By A. E. KEELING.

Brief Description of the Principal Places mentioned in Holy Scripture.

Bulmer's History of Joseph.

Bulmer's History of Moses.

Christianity Compared with Popery : A Lecture.

Daddy Longlegs and his White Heath Flower. By NELLIE CORNWALL.

Death of the Eldest Son (The). By CÆSAR MALAN.

Emily's Lessons ; Chapters in the Life of a Young Christian.

Fragments for Young People.

Freddie Cleminson.

Janie : A Flower from **South** Africa.

Jesus (History of). For Children. By W. MASON.

Little Nan's Victory. By A. E. COURTENAY.

Martin Luther (The Story of).

Precious Seed, and Little Sowers.

Recollections of Methodist Worthies. Foolscap 8vo, limp cloth.

Sailor's (A) Struggles for Eternal Life.

Saville (Jonathan), Memoirs of. By the Rev. F. A. WEST.

Soon and Safe : A Short **Life** well Spent.

Sunday Scholar's Guide (The). By the Rev. J. T. BARR.

The Wreck, Rescue, and Massacre : an Account of the Loss of the *Thomas King.*

Will Brown ; or, Saved at the Eleventh Hour. By the Rev. H. BUNTING.

Youthful Sufferer Glorified : **A** Memorial of Sarah Sands Hay.

Youthful Victor Crowned : A Sketch of Mr. C. JONES.

THE CROWN SERIES. *16mo. Cloth, gilt lettered. Coloured Frontispiece.* PRICE SIXPENCE.

1. A Kiss for a Blow : true Stories about Peace and War for Children.
2. Louis Henrie ; or, The Sister's Promise.
3. The Giants, and How to Fight Them.
4. Robert Dawson ; or, the Brave Spirit.
5. Jane Hudson, the American Girl.
6. The Jewish Twins. By Aunt FRIENDLY.
7. The Book of Beasts. 35 Illust.
8. The Book of Birds. 40 Illust.
9. Proud in Spirit.
10. Althea Norton.
11. Gertrude's Bible Lesson.
12. The Rose in the Desert.
13. The Little Black Hen.
14. Martha's Hymn.
15. Nettie Mathieson.
16. The Prince in Disguise.
17. The Children on the Plains.
18. The Babes in the Basket.
19. Richard Harvey ; or, Taking a Stand.
20. Kitty King : Lessons for Little Girls.
21. Nettie's **Mission.**
22. Little Margery.
23. Margery's City Home.
24. The Crossing Sweeper.
25. Rosy Conroy's Lessons.
26. Ned Dolan's Garret.
27. Little Henry and his Bearer.
28. The Woodman and his Dog.
29. Johnny : Lessons for Little Boys.
30. Pictures and Stories for the Little Ones.
31. A Story of the Sea : and other Incidents.
32. Aunt Lizzie's Talks about Remarkable Fishes. 40 Illusts.
33. Three Little Folks who Mind their own Business ; 25 Illustrations.
34. The Dairyman's Daughter.

The whole of the above thirty-four Sixpenny books are **also sold at Fourpence,** in Enamelled Covers.

PRICE SIXPENCE. *18mo. Cloth, gilt lettered.*

African Girls ; or, Leaves from the Journal of a Missionary's Widow.

Bunyan (John). The Story of his Life and Work told to Children. By E. M. C.

Celestine ; or, the Blind Woman of the Pastures.

Christ in Passion Week ; or, Our Lord's last Public Visit to Jerusslem.

Crown with Gems (The). A Call to Christian Usefulness.

Fifth of November ; Romish Plotting for Popish Ascendency.

Flower from Feejee. A Memoir of Mary Calvert.

Good Sea Captain (The). Life of Captain Robert Steward.

Grace the Preparation for Glory : Memoir of A. Hill. By Rev. J. RATTENBURY.

Joseph Peters, the Negro Slave.

Hattie and Nancy ; or, the Everlasting Love. A Book for Girls.

Held Down ; or, Why James did Not Prosper.

Matt Stubbs' Dream : A Christmas Story. By M. G. PEARSE.

Michael Faraday. A Book for Boys.

Our Lord's Public Ministry.

Risen Saviour (The).

St. Paul (Life of).

Seed for Waste Corners. By Rev. B. SMITH.

Sorrow on the Sea ; or, the Loss of the *Amazon*.

Street (A) I've Lived in. A Sabbath Morning Scene.

Three Naturalists : Stories of Linnæus, Cuvier, and Buffon.

Young Maid-Servants (A Book for). Gilt Edges.

PRICE FOURPENCE. *Enamelled Covers.*

Precious Seed, and Little Sowers.
Spoiling the Vines.
Rhoda, and Fire in the Soul.
The Fatherly Guide, and Fortune Telling.
Will Brown ; or, Saved at the Eleventh Hour.

Ancass, the Slave Preacher. By the Rev. H. BUNTING.
Bernard Palissy, the Huguenot Potter.
The Story of Martin Luther. By Rev. J. B. NORTON.
Little Nan's Victory.

The whole of the thirty-four books in the Crown Series at Sixpence are sold in Enamelled Covers at FOURPENCE each.

PRICE THREEPENCE. *Enamelled Covers.*

'The Ants' and 'The Conies.'
Concerning Play.
'The Kingly Breaker' and 'Sowing the Seed.'
'The Locusts' and 'The Spiders.'
Hattie and Nancy.
Michael Faraday.
John Bunyan. By E. M. C.

Three Naturalists : Stories of Linnæus, Cuvier, and Buffon.
Celestine ; or, the Blind Woman of the Pastures.
Held Down ; or, Why James didn't Prosper. By Rev. B. SMITH.
The Good Sea Captain. Life of Captain Robert Steward.

PRICE TWOPENCE. *Enamelled Covers.*

1. The Sun of Righteousness.
2. The Light of the World.
3. The Bright and Morning Star.
4. Jesus the Saviour.
5. Jesus the Way.
6. Jesus the Truth.
7. Jesus the Life.
8. Jesus the Vine.
9. The Plant of Renown.
10. Jesus the Shield.
11. Being and Doing Good. By the Rev. J. COLWELL.
12. Jessie Allen's Question.
13. Uncle John's Christmas Story.
14. The Pastor and the Schoolmaster.
15. Laura Gaywood.
16. In His Own Way. By KATE T. SIZER.
17. The Blind Girl and Her Brother. By A. E. COURTENAY.

The above Twopenny Books are also sold in Packets.
Packet No. 1, containing Nos. 1 to 6, Price 1/-
Packet No. 2, containing Nos. 7 to 12, Price 1/-

PRICE ONE PENNY. *Crown 16mo. Enamelled Covers. With Illustrations.*

1. The Woodman's **Daughter.** By LILLIE M.
2. The Young Pilgrim: the Story of Louis Jaulmes.
3. Isaac Watkin Lewis: a Life for the Little Ones. By MARK GUY PEARSE.
4. The History of a Green Silk Dress.
5. The Dutch Orphan: Story of John Harmsen.
6. Children Coming to Jesus. By Dr. CROOK.
7. Jesus Blessing the Children. By Dr. CROOK.
8. 'Under Her Wings.' By the Rev. T. CHAMPNESS.
9. 'The Scattered and Peeled Nation': a Word to the Young about the Jews.
10. Jessie Morecambe and Her Playmates.
11. The City of Beautiful People.
12. Ethel and Lily's School Treat. By R. R.

The above twelve books are also sold in a Packet, price 1/-

PRICE ONE HALFPENNY.

By MARK GUY PEARSE, LILLIE MONTFORT, RUTH ELLIOTT, and others. *Imperial 32mo. 16 pages. With Frontispiece.*

1. The New Scholar.
2. Is it beneath You?
3. James Elliott; or, the **Father's** House.
4. Rosa's Christmas Invitations.
5. A Woman's Ornaments.
6. 'Things Seen and Things not Seen.'
7. Will you be the Last?
8. 'After That?'
9. Christmas; or, the Birthday of Jesus.
10. The School Festival.
11. John's Teachers.
12. Whose Yoke do You Wear?
13. The Sweet Name of Jesus.
14. My Name; or, How shall I Know?
15. Annie's Conversion.
16. The Covenant Service.
17. The Chat in the Meadow.
18. The Wedding Garment.
19. 'Love Covereth all Sins.'
20. Is Lucy V—— Sincere?
21. He Saves the Lost.
22. The One Way.
23. Nora Grayson's **Dream.**
24. The Scripture Tickets.
25. 'Almost a Christian.'
26. 'Taken to Jesus.'
27. The New Year; or, Where shall I Begin?
28. The Book of Remembrance.
29. 'Shall we Meet Beyond the River?'
30. Found after Many Days.
31. Hugh Coventry's Thanksgiving.
32. Our Easter Hymn.
33. 'Eva's New Year's Gift.'
34. Noble Impulses.
35. Old Rosie. By MARK GUY PEARSE.
36. Nellie's Text Book.
37. How Dick Fell out of the Nest.
38. Dick's Kitten.
39. Why Dick Fell into the River.
40. What Dick Did with his Cake.
41. Dick's First Theft.
42. Dick's Revenge.
43. Alone on the Sea.
44. The Wonderful Lamp.
45. Not too Young to Understand.
46. Being a Missionary.
47. Willie Rowland's Decision.
48. 'Can it Mean Me?'
49. A Little Cake.
50. A Little Coat.
51. A Little Cloud.
52. The Two Brothers: Story of a Lie By MARK GUY PEARSE.

The above Series are also sold in Packets.
Packet No. 1 contains Nos. 1 to 24. Price 1/-
Packet No. 2 contains Nos. 25 to 48. Price 1/-

LONDON:
T. WOOLMER, 2, CASTLE STREET, CITY ROAD, E.C.